Deadly Eclipse

A CRIME THRILLER

TIFFANY C. JOHNSON

This is a work of fiction. Names, characters, places, events, and organizations are the products of the author's imagination or are used fictitiously. Any resemblance to actual persons, live or dead, businesses, events, locales, or organizations is entirely coincidental.

Text copyright © 2024 by Ocean Light Publishing
All rights reserved.
No part of this book may be reproduced, copied, or transmitted in any form or by any means, without direct written permission from the author or the publisher. The only exception is for brief quotations used in reviews or promotions.

Chapter 1

Early afternoon sunlight streamed through the tall windows of the Miami PD Narcotics Unit, creating beautiful patterns on Detective Elena Torres's desk. She was dressed in a fitted blouse and slim jeans, her dark hair pulled back in a ponytail as she sifted through a pile of reports. Suddenly, her phone vibrated. She saw that it was a call from the 12th District, which surprised her.

"Detective Torres."

"Detective Torres, this is Officer Johnson from the 12th District. I'm calling about your brother, Miguel. He's been arrested for drug possession."

"Miguel? Drugs? Are you sure?"

"Yes, ma'am. We found a small bag of cocaine on him during a routine stop. He's down here at the station."

"I'll be there right away." Elena could barely keep her thoughts straight as she hurried out of the headquarters.

Fifteen minutes later, Elena pushed open the door of the 12th District precinct, her heart pounding. The bustling station was a familiar sight, but today the weight of her brother's situation pressed down on her. She scanned the room, her eyes landing on the front desk where Desk Sergeant Jenkins was seated, typing away on his computer.

Jenkins looked up as she approached, a broad grin spreading across his face. He was a large man with a ruddy complexion. "Elena! Long time no see. What brings you here?"

Elena forced a smile. "Hey, Jenkins. I need to talk to the officer who arrested my brother, Miguel Torres. I heard he was brought in for possession."

Jenkins raised an eyebrow, as he leaned forward. "Your brother? Damn, Elena, I'm sorry to hear that. I'll get the officer for you. But first, when are we going to grab that beer you promised me?"

"I haven't forgotten, Jenkins. Let's catch up later after I deal with this."

"Of course. Let me see who handled the arrest." Jenkins tapped a few keys on his computer, scanning the screen. "Looks like it was Officer Johnson. I'll call him up for you."

Elena waited, her foot tapping anxiously against the tiled floor. A moment later, Officer Johnson appeared, a tall, lean man with sharp features and a no-nonsense demeanor. He nodded at Jenkins before turning to Elena. "You must be Detective Torres. I'm Officer Johnson. Let's talk about your brother."

"Yes, that's me. What happened? Why was Miguel arrested?"

Johnson gestured for her to follow him to a quieter corner of the precinct. "We picked him up during a routine patrol near the college campus. He had a small amount of drugs on him—cocaine. It wasn't much, but enough to bring him in for possession. He claims it's not his, but we need to follow protocol."

Elena's heart sank. Miguel, her younger brother, was a bright college student with a promising future. This wasn't like him. "Can I see him?"

"I'll take you to him. If there's anything you can tell us to help clear this up, it would be appreciated."

Elena followed Johnson down a series of corridors, the walls lined with faded posters and notices. When they reached the holding cells, Johnson unlocked a door and gestured for her to enter.

Miguel slumped on a bench, his curly hair disheveled, his hands clasped between his knees. His eyes, usually full of mischief, now held a shadow of something darker.

"Miguel, what the hell is going on?"

Miguel lifted his head slowly. "Elena, I'm so sorry."

"Drugs? Are you out of your mind?"

Miguel swallowed hard. "The drugs, they're not mine. Rico asked me to hold onto them. Just for a day, he said. I didn't think I'd get caught. I didn't mean for this to happen."

"Rico?" Elena's voice rose. "You know the kind of trouble he's mixed up in, Miguel. Do you think holding his stash is what? A favor between friends?"

"It's not like that. I didn't want to get involved, but—"

"Stop. I don't care about 'but'. You're smarter than this, or at least I thought you were. Given it's your first offense and the amount was small, you might get off with probation, but that's up to the judge."

"Officer Johnson, can we talk in private for a moment?" Elena asked.

"Sure, follow me."

In the hallway, Johnson turned to face Elena, his brow furrowed. "What's on your mind, Detective?"

Elena took a deep breath, steadying herself. "I need to ask a personal favor, Johnson. Miguel is an honor student at the University. He is my brother, and I know he made a mistake, but those drugs don't belong to him. The amount is small, and I believe he was set up."

Johnson crossed his arms. "Detective, you know the procedures. We have to follow protocol."

"I understand. But I'm asking you to let me take him home. I promise he won't leave town, and he'll be at his hearing. He's scared, and I don't want him to stay in a cell waiting for his hearing. Please, Johnson."

Johnson studied her for a moment and he knew Elena's reputation in the Narcotics Unit.

"Detective, I know your work and reputation in the Narcotics Unit, but you're putting me in a difficult position. However, I trust your judgment. If you're sure Miguel won't run, I'll process his release. But you have to make sure he's here for his hearing."

"Thank you, Johnson. I promise he'll be here. I'll personally ensure it."

"Alright. Let's get the paperwork started."

They walked back to the holding area, where Miguel sat anxiously on the bench.

"Officer Johnson is going to process your release," Elena said.

Miguel's shoulders sagged as the tension drained from his body. "Thank you, Officer. I'm so sorry for all of this."

"We'll talk about it at home. Right now, let's just get you out of here."

Johnson led them to the front desk, where he began the necessary paperwork. He handed Elena a clipboard. "Sign here, acknowledging that Miguel is being released into your custody and that he will appear for his hearing."

Elena signed the form and handed the clipboard back to Johnson. "Thank you."

"Just make sure he stays out of trouble, Detective."

"I will."

The squad car's backseat was a cramped space. Elena watched Miguel's shaky hands fumble with the seatbelt. Her movements were sharp and jerky as she revved the engine, her mind racing with all the warnings and lectures she had given him over the years. She questioned where she had gone wrong in reaching him, feeling like a failure as a sister.

"Elena, listen—" Miguel's voice broke the stifling silence.

"Look at me, Miguel. Drugs ruin lives. Do you remember Lisa Martinez? High school valedictorian, full ride to college?"

"Of course, I do."

"Dead at 22 because of an overdose. That's the reality. That could be you if you start to use drugs."

Miguel's gaze dropped.

"Now, promise me, no more favors, no more Rico, no more anything that even smells drug. Promise me, Miguel."

"I promise."

As they arrived at the modest apartment building that Miguel called home, he stepped out into the hot air. Elena followed, closing the distance between them with a few short steps. She placed her hands on his shoulders, the protective sister taking precedence over the hardened detective.

"I love you, little brother, even when I want to strangle you."

"I love you, too, Elena."

With a final look, Elena climbed back into the car, leaving Miguel standing there, watching her leave.

Chapter 2

Elena pushed open the glass doors of the Miami PD headquarters. The tension from her earlier confrontation with Miguel still clung to her, but she forced herself to focus on her tasks at hand. Detective Lucas Grant looked up from his desk as she entered their shared office. At 6'2" and with a strong, muscular build, Lucas was an imposing figure. His broad shoulders and chiseled jaw gave him a rugged, almost intimidating appearance, but his warm, green eyes softened his overall demeanor. His short, dark hair was neatly trimmed, and a faint stubble covered his jawline.

"Elena, everything alright?"

"Define 'alright'."

"How is your brother? I heard there was some trouble earlier."

"I guess words spread quickly in our circle." Elena collapsed into her chair. "Miguel has been released. Caught with a small amount of cocaine. Claimed it belonged to his friend Rico."

"That's tough. You believe him?"

"I don't know what to believe. He's my brother, Lucas. This is the first time he's been in trouble."

"He's lucky to have you looking out for him."

"But we have more pressing matters at hand." Elena tried to shut down the subject.

"Right." Lucas nodded and crossed his arms, the fabric of his shirt stretching over his biceps.

Elena's heart raced as she tried to keep her composure. The sight of Lucas' muscular frame always made her weak in the knees. She had made a vow to remain strictly professional with him, but every part of her yearned to run into his arms and never let go.

"Anything new come in while I was out?"

"Usual stuff," Lucas said. "Let's get through these reports first."

"Agreed."

Elena leaned back in her chair, massaging her temples as she looked up from the Sanchez case file. Across from her, Lucas was furiously typing on his computer. Their desks were positioned to face each other, an arrangement that fostered collaboration but also meant they couldn't escape each other's gaze.

"This Sanchez case is a nightmare," she said.

Lucas glanced up. "Tell me about it. A 15-year-old girl, dead from a drug overdose. It's tragic, and the school isn't exactly being forthcoming with information."

Elena flipped through the pages of the file. "Valeria Sanchez. Sophomore at Eastside High. Found in the girls' bathroom by a janitor after school hours. The toxicology report says it was heroin, laced with something else. Fentanyl, most likely."

"Her friends say she wasn't into drugs. Straight-A student, involved in sports and extracurriculars. No signs of trouble at home. It doesn't add up," Lucas shook his head.

"Exactly. But her locker had traces of the drugs. Someone must have planted them there, or she was hiding it from everyone."

Lucas frowned. "You think she was targeted? Maybe pressured into using?"

"It's possible. There's been a surge in drug activity around the school lately. We need to find out who's supplying these kids."

Lucas reached for his coffee, taking a sip before setting it down. "The principal mentioned a few students who've been in trouble for drug use. They all claim they got it from someone outside the school. A dealer is targeting the students."

Elena closed the file and leaned forward. "We need to talk to those kids again. A girl like Valeria doesn't just start using heroin out of the blue."

"Let's split up. You take the students, I'll talk to the staff again. Someone has to know more than they're letting on."

Before they could delve deeper into the conversation, the shrill ring of the phone cut through the air. Elena reached for the receiver. "Detective Torres speaking."

"Torres, Grant, my office. Now." The clipped tone of Captain Maria Rodriguez was unmistakable.

Elena replaced the receiver and exchanged a glance with Lucas. Wordlessly, they stood and made their way to the captain's office.

Captain Rodriguez was in her early fifties. Her dark hair was streaked with silver and pulled back into a tight bun. With a lean, athletic build, she exuded an air of authority and competence.

In her office, a large desk dominated the room, its surface meticulously tidy, with neatly stacked files and a computer monitor. Behind the desk, a wall of floor-to-ceiling shelves held binders, case files, and a few framed commendations. The only personal touch was a single photograph of her family on the corner of the desk.

"Detectives, come in," Rodriguez said as Elena and Lucas stepped into the office. She gestured for them to take a seat in the chairs opposite her desk. "Close the door. We've got a serious problem on our hands. There's been a recent surge in fentanyl-laced heroin overdoses across the city. The numbers are climbing, and we need to get ahead of this before it spirals further out of control."

"Do we have any leads on where the fentanyl is coming from?" Elena asked.

"We are not sure at this point. We've got a few sources indicating that a new supplier might be operating out of Little Havana. It's likely tied to one of the smaller gangs trying to make a name for themselves. We need to find out who they are and shut them down."

Lucas frowned. "Do we have any intel on which gangs might be involved?"

"Not yet," Rodriguez admitted. "We've got some informants on the ground who might have information. I want you two to start there. Shake the trees, see what falls out."

"We'll need to be discreet. If word gets out that we're investigating, the suppliers might go underground," Elena suggested.

"Exactly," Rodriguez said. "I trust you two to handle this with the necessary subtlety. Start with the usual suspects, but keep an open mind. This could be a new player, and they might not follow the old patterns."

"Understood. We'll get on it right away," Lucas said.

Rodriguez handed Lucas a folder containing the preliminary reports. "This is everything we have so far. I want daily updates on your progress. And remember, this is a priority case."

"Yes, Captain," Lucas said, taking the folder.

"Good. Dismissed."

As they left Rodriguez's office and walked down the hallway, Elena asked, "So, where do we start?"

Lucas opened the folder and quickly scanned the contents. "Let's begin with our informants in Little Havana."

Chapter 3

The sun shined brightly over the decaying industrial district. Lucas's heart began to race when he drove their Ford Explorer into the parking lot of a deserted warehouse. The building stood alone, engulfed by wild vegetation and piles of discarded junk, its windows shattered and walls covered in graffiti.

Elena stepped out of the car, her eyes scanning the perimeter. "Looks like we are the first on the scene." They spotted a cluster of teenage boys gathered at one corner of the parking lot, with their bikes neatly lined up beside them.

"I bet those are the ones who reported it," Elena said.

"Police!" Lucas announced as he flashed his badge.

"Hey, I'm Detective Torres, and this is Detective Grant. Can you tell us what happened?"

A lanky kid with a shock of bleached hair nodded. "We were just riding around, y'know? Then we saw this place and thought it'd be cool to check it out."

"Did you notice anything odd before you entered?" Lucas asked.

"No, sir," another teenager, bulkier with a nascent beard, piped up. "Was quiet as a grave."

"Until we found...them, the dead bodies," the lanky kid added, his eyes darting toward the door to the warehouse.

"Did you hear any gun shots?" Lucas asked.

"Nothing," the lanky biker said, swallowing hard.

"Did you touch anything at the scene?" Elena asked.

"God no," a third teenager interjected. "We wouldn't mess with something like this."

"Okay, we may need to speak with you further after processing the scene," Lucas said. "Stay here. Other police officers will arrive shortly. They will need to take your statements."

"Sure, detectives," the lanky one murmured, the others nodding in agreement.

Lucas and Elena walked toward the entrance of the warehouse, their footsteps resounding through the empty industrial area.

"Ready?" Lucas whispered as he pulled out his Glock 19. Elena nodded and drew her Sig Sauer P229 in response.

When Lucas pushed open the groaning metal doors, a wave of musty air greeted them. The interior of the warehouse was a cavernous expanse, shrouded in darkness that seemed impenetrable despite the sunny spring afternoon outside. Dust particles floated lazily in the beams of sunlight that pierced through the broken windows high above.

The vast space was cluttered with the remnants of a forgotten era. Rusted machinery stood like sentinels, their once-shiny surfaces now corroded and pitted. Broken crates and pallets were strewn haphazardly across the floor. Large, faded tarps hung from the ceiling, their tattered edges casting ghostly shadows.

Elena flicked on her flashlight, the beam cutting through the scene to reveal more details. Graffiti adorned the walls, a chaotic mix of tags and symbols. In one corner, a makeshift camp suggested recent human activity—discarded food wrappers, an old sleeping bag, and a charred circle of rocks indicating a small fire.

"What a mess," Elena breathed out.

"Watch your step," Lucas warned, his gaze tracking the bloodstains that marred the concrete floor, a gruesome trail leading further into the bowels of the warehouse.

"Looks fresh," she observed, squatting down to examine a dark smear. "Not more than a few hours old."

"Someone could still be here," Lucas said.

"I can see multiple bullet holes in the walls," Elena whispered.

"Left side," Elena whispered, motioning toward a stack of crates. Together, they moved with precision, each step measured to avoid contaminating the scene.

"More blood." Lucas pointed to a dark stain spreading out from beneath a nearby pallet.

"Fresh footprints." Elena used her flashlight to highlight a series of footprints leading away from the stain.

Then, the grisly tableau unfolded before them. Four bodies lay sprawled across the cold floor, limbs twisted at unnatural angles. It was the savagery of their deaths that clawed at Lucas' composure—their heads were missing, necks ending in ragged stumps.

"This is going to be a long day," Elena said.

Lucas knelt beside the first victim, his eyes narrowing as he studied the tattoos that curled over cold, lifeless skin.

"Look at this," Lucas called out to Elena, his finger hovering just above a tattoo of a serpent entwined around a set of scales—its fangs bared menacingly. "La Serpiente Balance. It's their mark."

Elena crouched beside him, her gaze tracing the lines of ink. "It's them alright. No mistaking the signature of the Scales Cartel. Looks like a drug deal gone wrong."

"These two definitely belong to the Scales Cartel and could have been the ones selling the drugs," Lucas said. "But what about the other two bodies without tattoos? They could have been buyers."

"Then who killed them?"

"It's possible that a third party attacked them and took the money and drugs," Lucas suggested.

"They were shot and decapitated. This seems to be a new pattern," Elena observed.

"Exactly. Remember the body we found at the beach last month? The same pattern," Lucas recalled.

Elena nodded in agreement before standing up.

"Whoever did this was sending a message. They were declaring war." Lucas's hand clenched into a fist.

"An escalation," Elena said. "This level of brutality is new. It's not just about turf or product anymore."

***

The coroner's van stopped at the entrance of the warehouse with a dull beep. A team of forensic experts in white suits and masks filed out, their equipment clinking softly as they entered the building.

"Over here," Lucas called out.

The team methodically snapped photos of the lifeless forms on the floor, preserved stray bullets into bags marked as evidence, and laid out body bags next to each victim.

"Lucas, make sure they check for any unusual markings or signs of struggle beyond the obvious," Elena said, as she jotted down notes on her pad.

Lucas turned to the coroner, who was kneeling by a body. "Dr. Miller, we're looking at possible gang-related executions. We need you to be thorough. Fingerprints, tattoos, fiber, and anything that doesn't belong."

"Will do, Detective Grant." Dr. Miller, a middle-aged man with tired eyes that had seen too much death, nodded solemnly. "We'll take extra care with the examination. I'll run toxicology and check for defensive wounds."

"Can you estimate the time of death?" Lucas asked.

"Judging from the body's temperature, I would say between 8:00 and 10:00 this morning."

Elena stepped closer. "If you can, identify the type of tool that was used for… decapitation."

"Of course, Detective Torres. I'll look into it and let you know the minute we find something that might help your investigation."

"Any timelines for when we can expect preliminary results?" Lucas asked.

"We can finish the basics within twelve hours, but toxicology reports will require more time," the coroner replied as his team began zipping up the body bags.

"That's great. We'll be back at the headquarters piecing together what we have so far. Please call us, day or night, if you get something," Elena said.

"You two be careful out there. It seems like things are spiraling out of control," the coroner added.

"We will." Lucas nodded to the departing coroner.

"We'll need to talk to our CIs, comb through every scrap of rumor and intel," Elena said.

"Time to pay Danny Ramirez a visit. If anyone has information about this new development, it's him," Lucas replied.

Chapter 4

The coroner's office was a sterile chamber, filled with the sharp smell of disinfectant and a faint hint of decomposition. Lucas' strong build slightly hunched as he gazed down at the corpse on the metal table, covered by a plain white sheet. Next to him, Elena maintained a poker face.

"Is this the body of Diego Rivera?" Lucas asked.

"Yes." Dr. Miller pulled back the sheet.

"No head, no easy ID," Elena whispered.

"Fortunately, his fingerprints match Diego's in our database," Miller said.

"Diego Rivera, 32 years old, was from Mexico. Diego immigrated to the United States at the age of 22 under a work visa. He initially worked in construction but later drifted into illegal activities. He was arrested three times for shoplifting, bar fight, and trafficking cocaine." Elena recited from the file she held in her hands.

"Diego is a confirmed member of the Scales Cartel," Lucas chimed in, pointing at the tattoo sprawling across the torso of the dead man—a serpent coiled around a set of scales.

"Discovering his identity is a significant breakthrough. Thank you, doc," Lucas added.

"You're welcome," Miller replied. He pointed at Diego and the body on the adjacent table. "These two were killed first." He then gestured toward the other two bodies without the serpent tattoos. "The killers kept those two alive for a few more hours before taking their lives." Dr. Miller walked over to the bodies without the tattoos. "Take a look at their hands," he said, motioning to the mutilated fingers. "Whoever did this took their time, torturing them. See? Several fingernails are missing."

Lucas leaned in closer, inspecting the ragged edges of skin where the nails had been forcibly removed. He could almost hear their screams echoing off the cold walls.

"Why were these two tortured, but not the other two?" Elena asked.

"I'm thinking they were trying to extract sensitive information, possibly a password. My theory is that these two were the buyers and they must have had some briefcase of money with them. Alternatively, they could have been subjected to torture to force them into transferring money to an offshore account." Lucus speculated.

"Look here." Dr. Miller gestured toward the necks of the corpses. Lucas and Elena stepped around to the other side of the table. The sight that met them sent a shiver down Lucas's spine, despite the years of horrors he'd seen on the job.

"Chopped off with a chainsaw, post-mortem," the coroner continued.

"Damn it," Lucas muttered.

"Whoever did this wanted to send a message," Elena added.

"A warning, maybe. These guys were soldiers. Someone's cleaning the house. Or starting a war," Lucas said.

"Maybe it's time to pay a visit to the Scales Cartel," Elena suggested.

Chapter 5

The blazing Miami sun beat down on the deserted car repair shop, its walls coated in a combination of rust and graffiti. The abandoned shop was located at the address listed on Diego Rivera's driver's license.

Lucas' hand rested on his holstered weapon as he strode toward the squad car, which had accompanied them to the location.

"Stay here," he instructed the patrolman in the driver's seat. "If we don't return within 20 minutes or you hear any gunshots, call for backup."

"Understood, sir," the patrolman responded.

With a wave of his hand, Lucas motioned for Elena to follow as they made their way toward the entrance.

Lucas knocked and pushed open the door. They stepped into the dimly lit interior. The air inside was thick with the scent of oil, gasoline, and grease, mingling with a faint smell of cigarette smoke. The main area of the shop was cluttered with an assortment of tools and car parts. An old wooden table ran along one side of the room, its surface covered in a thin layer of grime. Behind it, shelves lined the wall, filled with an assortment of car parts, cans of motor oil, and various other automotive supplies.

In the center of the shop, a large hydraulic lift held a battered sedan, its hood open and various parts strewn about. The lift's control panel was covered in greasy fingerprints, and a toolbox lay open nearby, its contents spilling onto the floor. The concrete floor was stained with oil and dotted with dark patches of dried blood.

Five young men lounged around the premises. Each of them bore a distinctive tattoo on their left forearm—a serpent entwined around a set of scales, the symbol of their allegiance.

A tall and muscular man with a shaved head was clearly the leader of the group. He leaned against a rusting car frame, his dark eyes scanning the detectives. His tattoo was larger than the others, the serpent's body wrapping around his bicep and extending down to his wrist.

Next to him stood a wiry young man with a shock of bleached blonde hair. His serpent tattoo was accompanied by various other designs, but the scales and serpent dominated his forearm, the ink black and fresh. He fiddled with a switchblade, flipping it open and closed, a smirk playing on his lips.

A third man, slightly older with a scruffy beard and a mane of dark hair tied back in a ponytail, lounged on the hood of a beat-up pickup truck. His tattoo was partially obscured by the sleeve of his T-shirt. He had a cigarette dangling from his lips, the smoke curling around his face.

The fourth man was a stocky young man with a shaved head and a thick neck, his arms crossed over his broad chest. His tattoo seemed almost to pulse with the movement of his muscles, the serpent appearing ready to strike at any moment.

The youngest of the group, a skinny kid barely out of his teens, stood nervously to the side, his hands shoved into the pockets of his hoodie. His tattoo was less elaborate, the lines still red and healing. He kept glancing at the leader, seeking silent approval or guidance.

"Police. We need to talk," Lucas announced.

"About what? Your last donut?" the leader of the group sneered, rising to meet them with a cocky swagger. The others laughed, a chorus of malice that did little to unsettle Lucas.

"About Diego Rivera," Elena interjected. "Does anyone here know Diego Rivera?"

The laughter died abruptly, replaced by a tense silence that hung in the air like humidity before a storm. The leader's expression hardened, the tattoos on his neck stretching tight.

"Never heard of him," he spat, crossing his arms.

"Cut the crap," Lucas growled, taking a step closer. His piercing gaze swept across the faces before him. "You want to play games, fine. But remember—your friends ended up headless. Do you know who killed Diego?"

Elena watched as the room's bravado faltered, the men exchanging uneasy glances.

"We're not leaving without something," Elena added.

"Get out," the young man with a shaved head growled, thumbs hooked into his belt loops. "Before we make you leave."

"Make me," Lucas challenged, the muscles in his jaw clenching. "Time's ticking and so is my patience."

Elena slid glossy photographs across the old wooden table. One by one, the young men leaned in, their hardened faces tightening at the sight of the mutilated bodies and the gruesome evidence of torture.

"Recognize them?" Elena's voice sliced through the heavy silence.

The skinny kid swallowed hard. His eyes darted from the photos to his companions.

Elena caught the flicker of fear and pressed on. "Your buddies were tortured, executed, decapitated. We want to catch the killers, just as much as you do."

"Look, we don't know nothing about no Phantom," the skinny kid stammered.

"Phantom?" Elena probed. "Who is Phantom? Did Phantom kill Diego Rivera?"

The room tensed, a collective breath held as the skinny kid's eyes fixed on a photo.

"Si, okay!" the kid burst out, "This is Diego. The Phantom—"

"Shut up, Leonardo!" the leader hissed, silencing him with a glare that could have cut glass.

"The Phantom is behind this, isn't he?" Elena asked softly, locking eyes with the one called Leonardo.

Leonardo nodded, just once, but it was enough.

"Let's go, Elena," Lucas said.

As they stepped out into the sweltering Miami sun, the warehouse door clanged shut behind them.

Chapter 6

As the sun began to set, Elena and Lucas arrived at Seabreeze Park. The soothing sound of waves caressing the shore filled the air, harmonizing with the distant calls of seagulls.

Elena stepped out of the car, taking a deep breath of the salty sea air. The park was a stretch of green that ran parallel to the sandy beach, dotted with palm trees swaying gently in the breeze. A path wound through the park, lined with benches and lampposts that would soon flicker to life as dusk settled in.

Families were packing up their picnics, and joggers were finishing their evening runs. The playground, a colorful array of swings and slides, was slowly emptying as parents gathered their children.

Elena and Lucas walked down the path, their footsteps muffled by the soft grass. They approached a secluded area of the park, where the path curved closer to the water. A small gazebo stood at the edge of the park, its white paint weathered. It was here that Danny "The Rat" Ramirez had agreed to meet them. The gazebo's benches were empty, save for a lone figure leaning against one of the columns, his silhouette sharp against the fading light.

Danny was a wiry man in his mid-thirties, his face lined with the weariness of someone who had seen too much. His dark hair was tousled by the breeze. As Elena and Lucas approached, he straightened, his eyes darting nervously around the park before settling on the detectives.

"You're late," Danny muttered.

Elena gave a brief nod. "Traffic. You have something for us?"

"Look, Danny, we need to know everything's tight here. No leaks," Lucas said.

"Leaks?" Danny scoffed. "You think I got a death wish? What I tell you stays in the shadows—just like me."

"Talk to us about The Phantom," Lucas said.

"Ah, The Phantom..." Danny sighed, scratching at his stubble. "That's a new player. I don't know who The Phantom is. That one's a ghost, man. Even in my circles—nothing. But there's someone who might be close to the smoke, if not the fire."

"Who?" Elena leaned in.

"Sofia Morales," Danny whispered. "Runs that swanky joint, La Luna Roja. The place is dripping with money, and not just the clean kind. She's got her fingers in a lot of pies, some may be linked to your specter friend."

"Connections or coincidences?" Lucas asked.

"Can't say for sure. But she throws parties where whispers flow like champagne. Old money, new drugs, and everything in between," Danny's eyes flickered with a knowing glint. "She knows people, and those people know things. If anyone's got a line on The Phantom, it's Sofia Morales."

Lucas's jaw clenched as Danny's words hung in the humid air between them.

"Alright, Danny," Lucas said, "what exactly is Morales' role in all this? Is she financing The Phantom? Providing a meeting place?"

"She's a facilitator. Her club's like neutral ground—everyone's welcome if they've got the cash or the clout."

"Neutral ground for who?" Elena interjected. "Are we talking about local thugs, international players?"

"Both. Her guest lists read like a who's who of the city's underbelly mixed with the cream of high society. If strings are being pulled in Miami, chances are they're tied to Sofia's little soirées."

"Does she have direct contact with The Phantom, or is she just another pawn in the game?" Lucas prodded.

"Hey, man, I don't know. But I'll tell you this—Sofia's no one's pawn. She plays the game too well. And word on the street is The Phantom has been looking for something big, something... lucrative."

"Any idea what that could be?" Elena asked.

"Rumors are all over the place. Could be a new drug hitting the streets soon, something potent. Or maybe a deal that's got all the major players buzzing. Whatever it is, I think Sofia's in the thick of it."

"Is Sofia The Phantom?" Lucas asked.

Danny shook his head. "I highly doubt it. Sofia has been a fixture in Miami for years. The Phantom, on the other hand, has only been wreaking havoc for the past six months."

The moon cast a silver glow over Seabreeze Park as Danny leaned against the weathered bench. "Sofia Morales has her fingers in more pies than you can imagine. A couple of months back, a shipment went south—a really bad scene. Everyone thought it would trigger a war, but Sofia? She steps in, and smooths everything over like she's spreading butter on toast."

Elena's dark eyes narrowed. "How'd she manage that?"

"Let's just say she's got dirt on everyone who's anyone—and those she doesn't, she charms. She hosted this little 'peace summit' at her club and rolled out the red carpet. By the end of the night, enemies were toasting like old pals. That woman could sell ice to Eskimos."

"Alright, Danny," Lucas nodded. "Keep your ear to the ground. We might need more from you soon."

"Always do, Detective Grant," Danny replied with a half-smile. "You know where to find me."

Lucas glanced over his shoulder, ensuring Danny had disappeared into the Miami night. He let out a slow breath, as he turned to Elena. "Thoughts?"

Elena paced alongside him, her eyes reflecting the myriad lights that dotted the skyline. "Danny's not the type to sell smoke. If he says Sofia Morales is our lead, I believe him."

"We start digging tomorrow. Surveillance, background checks, financials—the works. She must have a weak spot, and we're going to find it and use it." Lucas said, wrapping his arm around Elena.

"Watch it, Detective," Elena teased, playfully hitting his arm.

"My apologies, Detective. Can't seem to help myself." Lucas withdrew his hand.

"Apology accepted," Elena nudged her elbow against his, a warm smile on her face.

Chapter 7

Lucas heaved the solid black door open, and the pulsating beat of reggaeton music flooded out into the muggy Miami night. Vibrant neon lights flickered and danced, casting a rainbow of hues over the crowd of party guests, who moved together in sync on the dance floor at Sofia's nightclub.

"Stick close," Lucas muttered to Elena, as they weaved through the throngs.

A waitress approached them, balancing a tray in her hand. "Are you looking for someone?" she asked with a smile, her voice barely audible over the loud noise of the crowd.

Elena called out, "We're looking for Sofia Morales. Do you know where she is?"

The waitress nodded, gesturing for them to follow. She threaded through the club, her hips swaying to the rhythm of the music.

"Business or pleasure?" The waitress shouted over her shoulder.

"Official business." Lucas's response was curt.

They passed the dance floor where bodies moved in fluid motion.

"Ever been here before?" Elena's voice was barely audible.

"Never my scene," Lucas replied.

"Mine neither," Elena said.

After ascending the stairs, they arrived at a plain door guarded by a bulky man whose suit strained against his muscular frame. The waitress exchanged a brief word with him, and the guard assessed Lucas and Elena with a narrowed gaze before stepping aside.

"Good luck," the waitress said, as she turned and disappeared back into the chaos of the club.

Lucas and Elena entered Sofia's office, a spacious room that exuded luxury and sophistication. The walls were adorned with deep, rich hues of burgundy and gold. Soft lighting from elegant sconces and a crystal chandelier bathed the room in a golden glow, casting intricate patterns on the plush, cream-colored carpet.

A large, mahogany desk dominated the center of the room, its surface organized with a sleek laptop and a crystal decanter filled with amber liquid. Behind the desk, a high-backed leather chair stood like a throne. The back wall was lined with floor-to-ceiling windows that offered a panoramic view of the city skyline, the twinkling lights of Miami stretching out into the night.

To the left, a seating area was arranged with deep-cushioned sofas and armchairs upholstered in dark leather.

A glass coffee table sat between them, its surface gleaming under the chandelier's light. A bar cart stood nearby, stocked with top-shelf liquor and delicate glassware.

The right side of the office was an artistic showcase. Modern art pieces hung on the walls, while a sculptural vase with exotic flowers added a touch of nature to the opulent setting.

Sofia Morales sat behind her desk, exuding an air of confidence. Her blonde hair was perfectly styled, and she wore a sleek, designer dress that accentuated her curves.

"Hello, welcome to La Luna Roja. How can I assist you?"

"Good evening, Ms. Morales. I'm Detective Grant. This is Detective Torres. We need to ask you a few questions."

Sofia gestured to the seating area. "Please, make yourselves comfortable. Can I offer you a drink?"

Lucas shook his head politely. "We're here on business, Ms. Morales. It won't take long."

Sofia rose from her chair and moved to the seating area, inviting them to follow. "Of course. Let's get down to it, then."

As they settled into the luxurious armchairs, Sofia asked, "What brings Miami PD to my doorstep tonight?"

"Information," Lucas said. "The kind only someone with your... connections might have."

"Connections can be a double-edged sword, Detective. What makes you think I'll help you?"

"Because what we're dealing with affects us all," Elena interjected. "Lives are on the line."

Sofia regarded them for a long moment. "Ask your questions, Detectives."

Lucas met her gaze squarely. "Who is The Phantom?"

Sofia's jaw dropped, but she gathered herself quickly. "I'm not familiar with anyone who goes by that name."

Elena slid a manila envelope across the glass coffee table. "Take a look."

With a slight tilt of her chin, Sofia emptied the contents of the envelope onto the table. Glossy images spilled out like cards from a deck. She fanned out the photographs, her eyes scanning the brutality captured in still life.

Sofia took a sharp intake of breath as the color drained from her face.

"Who are these men?" Sofia's voice was a whisper.

"Members of the Scales Cartel, and a message."

"A message?" Sofia's hand hovered over the photos, her fingers trembling slightly.

"We believe it's a message from The Phantom." Elena watched as realization dawned on Sofia's face. "We need to know who The Phantom is."

Concern etched deep lines around Sofia's mouth and eyes in the dim light.

"Detectives, I—" Sofia began, then paused, collecting her thoughts. "This is not the kind of attention any businesswoman wants."

"This is not the type of news any detective wants to deliver," Elena said softly, "but here we are."

"Are you here to arrest me? Do you have a warrant?"

"We're not here to arrest you," Lucas clarified. "But if you don't assist us, we have the authority to thoroughly search your night club for drugs and illegal activities."

"I've never met The Phantom in person," Sofia said.

Elena leaned forward. "Sofia, we're not here to play games. The Phantom has started a war and we want to put an end to it. We need information, and we believe you have it."

"Detective Torres, I'm not sure what you expect me to—"

"Expect?" Elena cut her off. "I expect you to help us because it's the right thing to do. This kind of violence is bad for everyone and has to be stopped."

Sofia's lips parted, but no words came out. Instead, she swallowed hard.

"Look, I understand this is difficult," Lucas said. "But you've seen these streets, Sofia. You know how quickly things can turn bad."

"Bad doesn't begin to cover it," Sofia whispered.

Elena nodded. "Exactly. We can protect you, but only if you help us now."

Sofia's gaze flicked back to the photos, her red lips pressed into a tight line. After a moment that stretched out like a tightrope walker's pause, she looked up. "What do you need?"

"Names, places, anything that might connect The Phantom," Elena said.

Sofia leaned back, the leather of the armchair protesting with a soft creak. She lit a cigarette and inhaled deeply. As she exhaled, a plume of smoke danced toward the ceiling.

"The Phantom," she finally said. "His true identity remains a mystery. Rumor has it that he used to work in real estate before getting into the world of narcotics. He is very resourceful and has a lot of muscle."

"The Phantom imports materials and manufactures drugs in Miami. His newest product is called Eclipse," Sofia continued, tapping ash into a crystal tray. "He's determined to seek control of the drug market here in Miami and will eliminate anyone who stands in his way." Her lips curled into a sardonic smile.

"Can you give us names? Places? Anyone connected to The Phantom?" Elena asked, her pen poised over a small notebook she'd drawn from her pocket.

Sofia leaned in, her voice dropping to a whisper. "There's a warehouse on the outskirts. 1345 NE 22nd Street...rumors."

"Rumors?" Elena prompted.

"Late-night shipments. If The Phantom's crew is nesting, they're roosting there."

"Any idea who we should look for?" Lucas questioned.

"Vincent. I don't know his last name. I think he is in charge of that warehouse."

"Vincent," Elena repeated, etching the name into her notes. "Anything else?"

"Only that you didn't hear it from me," Sofia said, straightening up and casting a glance at the door. "The Phantom doesn't forgive those who step into his shadow."

"We were never here." Lucas stood up and offered a hand to Sofia.

"Just remember, Detective Grant, catching shadows can be as tricky as pinning down smoke." Sofia accepted his handshake with a firm grip. "Please leave my nightclub alone."

The pulsating beats of the nightclub reverberated through the floor as Lucas and Elena stepped out of Sofia's office. The dim, flashing lights and thrumming music made it hard to focus on anything but the immediate present.

Lucas's eyes were drawn to the dance floor. Amidst the writhing bodies, he spotted a familiar figure. His heart clenched as he recognized his ex-wife, Paisley, dancing passionately with a man he didn't recognize.

"Elena, hold on," Lucas said, his voice tense. "I need to handle something."

Elena followed his gaze and saw Paisley. "Lucas, maybe now isn't the best time."

Lucas made his way through the crowd, his jaw set in determination. He reached Paisley, tapping her on the shoulder. She turned, her smile fading as she recognized him.

"Lucas, what the hell are you doing here?"

"I could ask you the same thing, Paisley. Why aren't you at home taking care of Ava? She's only three, and she needs her mother."

Paisley rolled her eyes, taking a step back from her dance partner. "Fuck off, Lucas. I'm not in the mood for one of your lectures."

"This isn't a lecture, Paisley. This is about our daughter. You can't just abandon her to go party!"

Paisley's face twisted with anger. "Abandon her? I'm allowed to have a life, Lucas! You don't get to control me just because we have a kid together."

Lucas's fists clenched at his sides. "Ava needs stability. She needs her mother. This isn't about control, it's about responsibility."

Paisley crossed her arms. "You're one to talk about responsibility. Where were you when I needed help? Always off playing the hero, leaving me to pick up the pieces."

Lucas opened his mouth to retort, but Elena stepped in. She placed a firm hand on Lucas's arm, pulling him back. "Lucas, this isn't the place. Let's go."

Lucas resisted for a moment, his eyes locked on Paisley's, but then he let out a frustrated sigh and let Elena guide him away.

Once outside, Lucas took a deep breath, trying to calm the storm of emotions raging inside him.

"I just... I couldn't stand seeing her like that, knowing Ava was at home."

"I get it, Lucas. But getting into a public shouting match with Paisley isn't going to help Ava."

"You're right. It's just... it's hard."

"I know."

Lucas took another deep breath, steadying himself. "Okay. Let's get back to work."

"It's worth a trip here," Elena murmured.

"Let's just hope this lead doesn't end up like the others," Lucas replied.

"Either way, we're shaking the tree," Elena said.

"Let's see what falls out," Lucas added. They made their way to their unmarked car, minds racing with the possibilities of what lay ahead at 1345 NE 22nd Street.

Chapter 8

Lucas's grip on his Glock tightened as their police cruiser rolled to a stop, just shy of the waterfront warehouse's shadow. The warehouse stood tall against the night sky, its modern structure a stark contrast to the older buildings nearby.

A narrow road connected the warehouse to a dock. The road was lined with towering cargo containers, stacked high and forming a labyrinthine corridor leading up to the warehouse. The containers were painted in various colors and marked with shipping logos.

"Place looks dead," Elena muttered from the passenger seat.

"Too dead. Alright, let's gear up. Remember, a shipment is coming in tonight. We need to be quick and quiet." Lucas addressed the team through their earpieces as he stepped out of the car. The rest of their unit, clad in tactical vests, emerged from the vehicles behind them.

The glow of their flashlights cut through the darkness and the air carried the faint scent of salt and diesel. The warehouse was a fortress of steel and glass. Large, reinforced doors marked the entrance, with smaller side doors likely used for quick exits. High windows ran along the upper level, their glass panes glinting under the moonlight. There were security cameras, but the team had ensured they were temporarily disabled for this operation.

"Feel that?" Elena's hand signaled for the team to halt. Her dark brown eyes met Lucas's. *Something wasn't right.*

"Yeah," Lucas affirmed, his piercing gaze scanning the upper windows. "It's too quiet—no guards, no lookouts, nothing. It's like they're expecting us."

"Or waiting for us," Elena added.

"Keep your eyes peeled. Let's move," Lucas ordered and signaled the team forward with a hand gesture.

Lucas felt the first bullet whiz past his ear, a sinister whisper that shattered the silence. "Snipers!" he barked, instinctively diving for cover.

"Get down!" Elena's voice echoed his urgency, as the team dove for cover behind a stack of cargo containers.

"Where are they?" one of the policemen shouted.

Bullets whizzed past, pinging off metal and concrete.

"Atop the cargo containers and in the surrounding buildings!" Lucas called out, his eyes darting to the rooftops, trying to spot muzzle flashes or glints of scopes. He cursed under his breath; the snipers had them pinned like fish in a barrel.

"Stay low!" Elena commanded and dragged a disoriented rookie officer into the scant shelter offered by a cargo container.

"Lucas, we need a plan!" she yelled over the chaos.

Lucas fumbled for his radio. "Captain Rodriguez, this is Lucas. We're under heavy fire outside the warehouse. Snipers on top of containers and in surrounding buildings. We need backup immediately!"

The radio crackled with static before Rodriguez's voice came through. "Hang tight, Lucas. The SWAT team is on their way. Hold your position."

"Get ready to lay down suppressive fire when I give the signal," Lucas commanded his team. "We have to move away from the entrance. We're trapped here."

"Copy that," Elena acknowledged, signaling to the others. The team huddled closer, their hands tight on their weapons, waiting for the signal.

"Three, two, one—now!" Lucas's command cut through the air, followed by a cacophony of gunfire from their side.

Glass exploded above them, raining down like a deadly hailstorm as windows burst from sniper fire. Shards glittered in the moonlight, embedding themselves into the walls and the ground, creating a treacherous landscape of reflections.

"Damn it, we're boxed in!" one officer cried out, as he ducked a shard that embedded itself into the wall where his head was moments before.

"Move!" Lucas propelled Elena toward a stack of containers.

A scream cut through the chaos as an officer went down, clutching his shoulder where a bullet had struck. Blood seeped through his fingers, his face contorted in pain. "I'm hit!"

"Hold on, we've got you!" Lucas and Elena crawled toward the injured officer, bullets ricocheting off the container inches from their heads.

Reaching the officer, Lucas and Elena grabbed him under his arms, dragging him behind a container. "Stay with us," Elena urged, applying pressure to the wound to stem the bleeding. The officer's breathing was ragged, his eyes wide with shock.

"Snipers... two, maybe three positions," Elena panted, squinting into the dim silhouettes of surrounding buildings.

"Can you see them?" Lucas asked.

"Negative. They're ghosting us."

"We need to wait for the SWAT—" But before Lucas could finish, a deafening roar cut him off.

The air seemed to rupture as an explosion tore through the warehouse. The blast wave hit Lucas and Elena like a physical force, throwing both of them to the ground. Heat seared their skin, and a rain of fire and debris blanketed the area. Lucas felt the ground shudder beneath him as if the earth itself was rebelling against such violence.

"Lucas!" Elena's shout reached him through the ringing in his ears. Her silhouette was barely visible through the thick smoke and dancing flames that had transformed the night into a vision of hell.

"Here!" he choked out, coughing from the dust and fumes.

Lucas's ears were still ringing when the pained cries cut through the haze of his disorientation. He turned, squinting through the smoke, and saw two uniformed bodies on the ground, writhing in agony. One clutched his leg, a shard of shrapnel embedded deep into the flesh, while the other tried to stem the flow of blood from a gash across his arm.

Thankfully, the SWAT team had finally arrived and it seemed that the sniper's shots had ceased.

"We need an ambulance! Officers down!" Elena barked into her radio. She was already by their side, ripping open a first aid kit. "Hang in there, guys. Help is on the way."

Lucas moved to assist, but his mind raced, piecing together the grim puzzle. Silence before the storm, a sniper's perfect shot, a warehouse rigged to blow—the trap had snapped shut with lethal efficiency, and they had walked right into it.

"Damn it, Elena," Lucas growled, crouching beside her. "Sofia played us."

"Looks that way," Elena agreed. "But why? Does she really believe she can get away with this?"

"Maybe to throw suspicion off herself. Or maybe The Phantom got to her, made her an offer she couldn't refuse."

"Or a threat she couldn't escape," Elena added.

"Either way," Lucas said, helping her to lift one of the injured men onto an improvised stretcher, "we're up against someone who knows how to manipulate us, use our own moves against us."

"We will make them regret ever starting this game," Elena said.

Chapter 9

Lucas's phone vibrated in his pocket. He snatched it out, pressing it to his ear, and barked into the receiver, "Lucas."

"Lucas," came the voice of Captain Rodriguez. "You need to get to Sofia Morales' nightclub, now."

"Captain, we just—" Lucas began, but Rodriguez cut him off.

"Listen to me, Lucas. There's been a development. I can't talk over the air. Just get there!"

"Copy that," Lucas said tersely, snapping the phone shut. He glanced at Elena. "Captain wants us at Sofia's nightclub. Says it's urgent."

"Then we go." Elena's eyes flickered with unspoken questions, but she didn't voice them.

Together, they sprinted to the car. They peeled away from the warehouse, sirens screaming into the night.

"Whatever it is, it's big," Lucas said, swerving around a stalled taxi.

"Sofia setting us up, the ambush—what's waiting for us at that club?"

"Only one way to find out." Lucas' foot pressed harder against the accelerator, the car hurtling forward like a missile.

"If this is another setup..." Elena cautioned, checking her sidearm.

"Then we'll deal with it."

Thirty minutes later, Lucas and Elena pulled up to Sofia's nightclub. The usual buzz of the night was replaced with a somber stillness. The entrance was warded off by yellow police tape fluttering in the breeze. Two uniformed officers stood guard and kept curious onlookers at bay, their expressions grave.

Elena flashed her badge at the officers, and they lifted the tape to let her and Lucas pass. The nightclub's interior was a stark contrast to its usual vibrant, pulsating atmosphere. The dance floor was deserted, and the music had been silenced. A few officers were scattered throughout the space, interviewing employees whose faces were pale.

"Detectives," an officer greeted them. "Follow me. It's bad."

Lucas and Elena followed the officer up the stairs to Sofia's office. As they reached the top of the stairs, the officer paused, gesturing to a shadowed corner near the office door. Lucas and Elena's flashlights illuminated Sofia's bodyguard, a hulking figure slumped against the wall. Blood had pooled beneath him, a dark, sticky mess spreading out from the fatal wound in his head. The single, precise shot indicated the use of a silencer, the telltale sign of a professional hit.

"Damn," Lucas muttered, crouching beside the body. The bodyguard's face was frozen in a final expression of surprise, his eyes still open, staring blankly ahead. "They took him out clean. He didn't even have time to draw his weapon."

Elena knelt beside Lucas, examining the scene. "Looks like he was standing guard. He never saw it coming. Whoever did this knew exactly what they were doing."

The officer cleared his throat, drawing their attention. "It gets worse inside."

Lucas and Elena exchanged a grim look before rising to their feet. "Let's see it," Lucas said.

The officer pushed open the door to Sofia's office, and they stepped inside. The air was thick with the metallic scent of blood, mingling with the remnants of Sofia's perfume. Sofia's office was now a blood-soaked crime scene. The rich burgundy and gold walls were splattered with dark, congealed blood. The plush cream-colored carpet was stained a deep crimson.

Sofia's grand mahogany desk was in disarray. The sleek laptop was knocked to the floor, its screen shattered. The crystal decanter lay on its side, its contents spilled and mingling with the blood. The high-backed leather chair was toppled over, its surface marred by deep, violent slashes.

The most chilling detail was the message scrawled on the wall behind the desk. Written in bold, red strokes with lipstick, the word "SNITCH" screamed out. The lipstick, a bright crimson, stood out vividly against the gold wallpaper, the letters jagged and hurried.

Sofia's body lay slumped against the desk, her head nowhere to be found. Her elegant dress was torn, and her hands were bound with coarse rope. Blood pooled around her body, seeping into the carpet and spreading out in a macabre halo.

Elena's stomach churned at the sight. "Jesus," she whispered.

"This is a message to anyone thinking about crossing them," Lucas said.

The officer who had led them in cleared his throat, his face pale. "We found the lipstick in her hand. It looks like they forced her to write the message before... before they finished her off."

Elena knelt beside Sofia's body, examining the ropes and the bruises on her wrists. "They tortured her. This wasn't just about killing her. They wanted to make her suffer."

Lucas turned his attention to the room, his eyes scanning for any clues. "We need to find out who did this, and we need to find her head."

"How did they find out she was talking to us?"

"This place could be bugged. We need the tech team to sweep for any listening devices," Lucas said.

"Or someone on the dance floor saw us and recognized us," Elena replied.

"It's too easy these days with facial recognition technology." Lucas sighed.

"I can't believe we failed to protect her. How did things escalate so quickly?" Elena said. "Whoever did this wanted us to see it. To warn us."

"Message received," Lucas replied, his jaw tightening. "Let's call it in."

"This is Lucas Grant. We need a forensics team and a tech team at the La Luna Roja nightclub, immediately," he spoke into his radio.

"Copy that, Detective. What's your situation?" crackled the dispatcher's voice.

"Homicide. It's bad," he replied curtly.

"Let's step out. Give the techs space to work," Lucas suggested, moving toward the door.

They stepped out into the humid Miami night, the pulsing red and blue lights of arriving squad cars painting the scene in surreal strokes.

"Lucas, Elena, what's the status?" barked Captain Rodriguez as she approached them, her expression grim.

"Captain, The Phantom—this is their doing. It's a clear message to us, to anyone who dares work with us," Lucas reported.

"Finding The Phantom is now our main focus," declared Rodriguez. "I'll make sure you have additional assistance."

"Does the DEA have any information on The Phantom?" Elena asked.

"I'll look into it. Lucas, Elena, you've had a long day. Take a break. We'll regroup and brief in the morning," Captain Rodriguez directed, turning to address the officers securing the perimeter.

Chapter 10

The muffled hum of downtown Miami filtered through the blinds, setting a stark contrast to the tense silence that stifled the conference room. Captain Rodriguez leaned against the edge of the projector table, arms folded. Her gaze swept over the room with the precision of a general assessing her troops.

"Lucas, Elena," she began, "I'm adding Detective Tom Yates and Officer Baxter Bradley to your task force."

Lucas's eyes flickered toward Tom, a sturdy figure leaning casually against the doorframe. His buzz cut reflected the fluorescent light. Officer Baxter Bradley sat to the side, fresh-faced and eager, his fingers tapping on the table like a silent drumbeat of anticipation.

"Tom's record speaks for itself," Rodriguez continued, "and Baxter here is a wiz with any tech you throw at him."

"Welcome aboard." Lucas offered a hand to each in turn.

"Thanks, man." Tom grinned.

"Happy to help," Baxter chimed in.

Rodriguez pushed off from the table and stood straight. "We took a hit with that warehouse ambush; evidence up in smoke, leads turned to ash. We need to regroup and rethink."

"Start from scratch," Elena added.

"Exactly," Rodriguez affirmed. "This isn't just about finding a needle in a haystack anymore. It's about weaving back together the pieces of a haystack that's been burned to the ground."

"Which means we're going back to basics," Lucas said. "Street level, informants, surveillance—whatever it takes."

"Every resource at your disposal. You're the best of the best. That's why you're on this task force. I have confidence in you," Rodriguez said. She glanced at her watch and straightened her uniform, a subtle sign that her part in this meeting was over. With a nod, she strode out.

Lucas leaned forward. "Let's start with Sofia Morales's murder last night. We have witnesses who saw a group of five men dressed in black and baseball caps entering the nightclub through the back door. They carried heavy bags, most likely weapons and equipment. This was a coordinated hit."

Elena nodded, her brow furrowed in thought. "The tech team found something disturbing. Sofia's office was bugged. The Phantom must have a recording of our earlier conversation with Sofia. They knew exactly what was going on."

Tom leaned back in his chair. "So they knew we were closing in. This was their way of eliminating a threat."

"We need to trace where that bug came from. If we can figure out who planted it, we might be able to link it back to The Phantom's crew," Baxter said.

"Agreed. But we also need to focus on identifying the five men who carried out the hit. They're our immediate suspects, and we need to find them before they disappear," Lucas added.

"Do we have any footage from the security cameras in Sofia's nightclub from last night?" Baxter asked.

Elena shook her head. "The killers destroyed all the security camera footage. They knew exactly what they were doing, making sure we had no visual evidence to work with."

Tom leaned forward, his brow furrowed. "What about the witnesses? Can they describe what the killers look like?"

Lucas sighed, rubbing his temples. "Unfortunately, no. The killers lowered their baseball caps so that nobody saw their faces clearly. All we know is that the five men were of average height and moved like trained military."

Baxter nodded slowly. "So we're dealing with professionals. They knew how to avoid detection and covered their tracks well."

Elena pulled out a map of the nightclub and its surroundings, spreading it out on the table. "We need to find another angle. If they were so meticulous about destroying the footage, they might have overlooked something else. Maybe there's a clue in the few seconds before the cameras were disabled. Let's also look at the area around the nightclub. If they entered through the back, they must have had a getaway plan. We need to check all surveillance footage from nearby businesses and traffic cameras."

Tom leaned in, tracing his finger along the map. "There's an alleyway behind the nightclub that leads to a parking lot. It's secluded, perfect for their escape. We should check there first."

"We also need to look into Sofia's connections," Lucas said. "Who might have wanted her dead? The Phantom had a reason, but we need to consider all angles. Who benefits from her death?"

"And we should interview everyone who was in the nightclub last night. Someone must have seen or heard something that could give us a lead," Tom added.

"Ok, now let's talk about Vincent. He ambushed us at the warehouse," Lucas slammed his palm against the conference room table, a resounding thud echoing off the walls. "He is out there, somewhere. Sofia gave us that much before—before it all went down."

"Vincent is a ghost. Without the warehouse to comb through for leads. It's like he vanished into thin air," Elena said.

"Then we'll pull him back out of it." Lucas stood up so abruptly that his chair screeched behind him.

"We need a name, a face—anything. We turn over every stone, shake down every informant," Tom said.

Lucas eyed Tom for a moment before nodding slowly. "Good point, Tom. We will interview every employee of

Sofia's nightclub to see if anyone knows of any Vincent. Do we have other ways to reveal Vincent's identity?"

Elena rubbed at her temple. "Without a last name, it's difficult."

"Not necessarily," Baxter interjected. He gestured toward the array of screens on the wall. "I can start mining through databases, and cross-reference any Vincents with known associates from Sofia's case files. There's also facial recognition—"

"Facial recognition?" Elena echoed skeptically. "We don't know what the guy looks like."

"Yet," Baxter countered. "We have footage from around the warehouse before the explosion, right? Traffic cams, local businesses. If Vincent worked there, we'll find his face and run it through every database we've got."

"Surveillance footage," Tom murmured. "With the right enhancement algorithms, we might get something usable."

"Exactly. I've been working on this new pattern recognition software. It could help us predict his next moves based on behavior modeling," Baxter said.

"Behavior modeling. That's... pretty cutting edge, Baxter," Lucas said.

"Can you do it?" Elena asked.

"Give me access to the data, and I'll make it happen," Baxter replied.

"Alright," Lucas said, clapping his hands together. "Baxter, you take point on tech. Tom, you ask your CIs for information. Elena and I go talk to employees of Sofia's nightclub."

"You got it, boss," Baxter said.

Chapter 11

Under the bright sun of a Saturday morning, Lucas arrived at his ex-wife Paisley's apartment complex. He took a deep breath, steeling himself for the inevitable interaction with Paisley. He was here for one reason only: to spend some quality time with his daughter, Ava.

Lucas knocked on the door, and after a few moments, Paisley answered. She looked tired but managed a small smile.

"Morning, Lucas," she said, stepping aside to let him in. "Ava's just finishing breakfast."

"Thanks, Paisley."

Ava came running out of the kitchen, her face lighting up when she saw Lucas. "Daddy!" she squealed, launching herself into his arms.

Lucas scooped her up. "Hey there, princess! Ready for our adventure?"

Ava nodded enthusiastically. "Yes! Where are we going?"

"It's a surprise," Lucas said, tapping her nose playfully. "I think you're going to love it."

He grabbed her small backpack, already packed with snacks and a change of clothes, and headed for the door. "We'll be back by dinner," he said to Paisley.

"Have fun," Paisley said.

As Lucas buckled Ava into her car seat, he could see her excitement bubbling over.

"Daddy, tell me where we're going!"

"Okay, okay. We're going to Jungle Island. How does that sound?"

Ava's eyes widened in delight. "Yay! I love Jungle Island!"

***

Lucas and Ava strolled through Jungle Island, as the sounds of chirping birds filled the air.

"Look, Daddy! The petting zoo!" Ava exclaimed, her tiny hand pointing eagerly toward a fenced-in area bustling with children and animals.

"Alright, princess. Let's go."

When they entered the petting zoo, Ava's eyes widened with delight. A group of goats, rabbits, and even a few small lambs roamed the enclosure, welcoming gentle pets and treats from excited children.

Ava dashed toward two goats, a giggle escaping her lips as they nuzzled her hand, looking for food. Lucas handed Ava a small cup of feed, and she eagerly began distributing the pellets.

"Daddy, they're so soft!" Ava said, her eyes sparkling as she petted a fluffy rabbit. The rabbit's nose twitched as it sniffed her hand, and she giggled again.

Lucas watched her, a soft smile on his face.

"Can I take one home, Daddy?" Ava asked as she cuddled a fluffy rabbit.

Lucas chuckled, kneeling beside her. "I wish we could, sweetheart, but these little guys belong here. How about we come to visit them whenever you want?"

Ava pouted for a moment, then brightened up. "Okay! Only if I can feed them every time."

"You've got a deal," Lucas said, ruffling her hair. "Let's give this little one some more food."

"Daddy, look!" Ava called, holding up a tiny, fluffy chick. "Isn't it cute?"

"Very cute, just like you."

Ava beamed, carefully placing the chick back in its pen. She ran back to Lucas, wrapping her arms around his leg. "I love you, Daddy."

Lucas scooped her up, holding her close. "I love you too, princess."

The sun climbed higher in the sky when Lucas and Ava made their way to the bird sanctuary. The air was alive with the vibrant calls of parrots and macaws, the colorful birds flitting from branch to branch in the lush greenery.

"Daddy, look at that one!" she exclaimed, pointing to a scarlet macaw perched high on a branch. "It's so pretty!"

"It sure is. Do you know what kind of bird that is?"

Ava shook her head. "No, what is it?"

"That's a scarlet macaw. They're known for their bright red feathers and are very smart birds."

Ava tried to mimic the macaw's call, her high-pitched attempt drawing the attention of the bird, which tilted its head curiously. Lucas couldn't help but laugh.

"Look, Daddy! It's listening to me!"

"They must think you're one of them. Why don't we see if we can find some more friends to talk to?"

After exploring the bird sanctuary, they found a quiet spot in one of the park's picnic areas. Lucas spread out a blanket under the shade of a large tree, its branches providing a cool respite from the midday sun. He unpacked their lunch, laying out sandwiches, fresh fruit, and a few cookies.

"Come here, Ava. Let's have some lunch."

Ava skipped over, plopping down with a big smile. "I'm hungry, Daddy!"

They settled in, enjoying the simple meal.

"The goats were so funny," Ava said, her mouth full. "They kept trying to eat my hair!"

Lucas handed her a napkin. "Well, your hair does look pretty tasty."

"And the rabbits were so soft!"

Ava was munching on a slice of watermelon, when Lucas's phone buzzed.

He pulled it out and saw a message from Elena. It was a picture of her, beaming with pride, as she crossed the finish line of a 5K race in Miami. She looked radiant, her athletic frame glistening with sweat.

"Look, Ava," Lucas said, showing her the picture. "Elena just finished a race. Doesn't she look happy?"

Ava peered at the photo, her eyes wide with curiosity. "Is she your girlfriend, Daddy?"

Lucas chuckled. "No, sweetheart. Elena is just my partner at work. We solve cases together."

Ava tilted her head, clearly pondering something. "But you like her, right? You should ask her out, Daddy."

Lucas ruffled Ava's hair. "Is that so? Why do you think I should date her?"

Ava shrugged. "Because she's nice and you smile when you talk about her."

Lucas couldn't help but smile at his daughter's observation. "You're quite the matchmaker, aren't you?"

Ava nodded enthusiastically, taking another bite of her watermelon. "Yep! And I think Elena likes you too."

Lucas shook his head, amused. "Well, I appreciate the advice, love guru. But sometimes grown-ups are just friends, and that's okay too."

Ava gave him a knowing look. "Okay, Daddy. But if you ever need help, just ask me."

"I'll remember that. Now, how about we go see the tigers after lunch? I heard they're pretty amazing."

"Yes! I want to see the tigers!"

Chapter 12

Lucas and Elena stepped into the office. Captain Rodriguez sat behind her desk, her expression serious as she gestured for them to sit.

"Detectives, this is Agent Calvin Jackson from the DEA," Rodriguez said.

Agent Jackson stood and extended his hand in greeting. Standing at six feet with a muscular build, he could handle himself in a fight. His dark skin contrasted with his neatly pressed white dress shirt, and his close-cropped hair was flecked with hints of gray.

"Agent Jackson." Elena offered her hand, her eyes sizing him up.

"Please, call me Calvin," he replied, accepting the handshake. "I've heard good things about you both."

"Let's cut to the chase." Lucas' gaze locked onto Calvin. "What brings the DEA to our backyard?"

"Direct. I like that. We have reasons to believe that Gabriel Sandoval, the real estate mogul, has ties with The

Phantom. We've been watching him for over six months now."

"Gabriel Sandoval, the real estate tycoon?" Surprise etched Elena's face. "He's practically Miami royalty. It didn't make sense that he would want to involve himself in the drug business."

"Gabriel is ex-marine. The FBI has been keeping an eye on his commercial real estate ventures, and Gabriel has been struggling for several years now. In fact, he almost declared bankruptcy last year," Calvin explained. "But suddenly, within the past three to six months, there's been a huge turnaround. His bank accounts are overflowing with cash. And where there's smoke..."

"There's usually a fire," Lucas finished for him.

"Exactly. We've got preliminary evidence linking Gabriel to drug trafficking and The Phantom, but we need more to make it stick."

"Count us in." Elena exchanged a look with Lucas. "We have at least five dead bodies that are linked to The Phantom."

"Good. Because we're going to need all the help we can get," Calvin said. He leaned back against the edge of Rodriguez's desk, folding his arms. "As it happens, Gabriel is playing host this very afternoon. High-profile social event at his private golf course. The perfect opportunity for you two to get a closer look."

"Cozy up to Miami's elite?" Elena quipped.

"Sounds good," Rodriguez said. "If you can blend in, you might pick up something useful."

Lucas rubbed his chin thoughtfully. "We'll need a cover story."

"Rich couple looking to settle down by the ocean?" Elena suggested.

"Sounds like we're going house hunting, then," Lucas said.

"Keep it convincing," Calvin warned. "Gabriel's no fool. He's got eyes everywhere."

"No one looks twice at a couple in love with the view," Elena assured him.

"Let's hope the view includes Gabriel letting slip something about The Phantom," Lucas added.

"Get in, mingle, get out. And don't forget to enjoy the canapés," Calvin said, a wry smile breaking his professional demeanor.

"Canapés and criminals," Elena echoed, a playful smirk lighting up her face as she moved toward the door. "My kind of party."

Chapter 13

Lucas checked his watch as the silver Aston Martin pulled up to Gabriel Sandoval's private golf course. The entrance was marked by grand wrought-iron gates, which swung open to reveal a long, winding driveway lined with manicured hedges and towering palm trees.

When Lucas and Elena drove toward the clubhouse, the sprawling beauty of the golf course unfolded before them. The emerald fairways stretched out in undulating waves. Sand traps and water hazards dotted the landscape, adding both challenge and charm to the scene.

The clubhouse was a blend of modern elegance and classic luxury. Its walls were made of white stucco, accented with dark wooden beams and large glass windows that offered panoramic views of the course and the ocean beyond. A spacious terrace wrapped around the building, filled with clusters of elegantly dressed guests mingling under large, cream-colored umbrellas.

Lucas adjusted his tailored suit jacket. "Ten minutes ahead of schedule."

"Early bird catches the worm—or in our case, the intel," Elena replied from the passenger seat, slipping on a pair of oversized sunglasses.

"Let's hope this worm isn't buried too deep," Lucas murmured as he parked the car and stepped out into the balmy air. They walked side by side, a couple seemingly intoxicated by the allure of wealth. The sounds of polite conversation and soft laughter reached their ears, mingling with the gentle clinking of glasses. Waitstaff in crisp white uniforms moved gracefully among the guests, offering trays of champagne flutes and hors d'oeuvres.

"Remember, we're supposed to be impressed by the ocean front view," Elena whispered, linking her arm through his as they approached a group of guests lounging near an ornate fountain.

"Ah, I believe I've seen you two at the Harper's Bazaar event last fall, haven't I?" a woman with a champagne flute in hand asked.

"Indeed, it was unforgettable," Lucas responded, offering a charming smile that didn't quite reach his eyes. "But the oceanfront properties here might just eclipse that memory."

"Gabriel has outdone himself with this development," the woman cooed. "If you're looking to buy, you've chosen a perfect day for it."

"Everything about today seems perfect," Elena added.

They made their way toward the clubhouse, their shoes crunching softly on the gravel path. The air was fragrant with the scent of blooming flowers from the gardens that framed the course.

Inside the clubhouse, crystal chandeliers hung from the high ceilings, casting a warm glow over the polished marble floors and rich mahogany furnishings. The walls were adorned with art pieces and photographs of Gabriel's many achievements, both in business and philanthropy.

Lucas and Elena weaved through the throng of guests, their eyes observing the interactions and exchanges around them. The attendees were a mix of high-profile figures—business moguls, celebrities, politicians, and socialites, all gathered to bask in the luxury of Gabriel's hospitality.

Lucas nudged Elena subtly and inclined his head toward a figure commanding attention at the center of a group. Gabriel Sandoval was in his fifties, with a lean, muscular build that spoke of his years as a Marine. His salt-and-pepper hair was neatly styled, and his chiseled features were accentuated by a strong jawline and piercing blue eyes. He wore a perfectly tailored black suit.

"Showtime," Lucas murmured under his breath.

"We're just a couple admiring the view," Elena whispered back, adjusting the elegant scarf that draped over her shoulders.

They edged closer to the circle surrounding Gabriel. A waiter passed by, and Lucas plucked two flutes of champagne from his tray, handing one to Elena with a sweet smile.

"Thank you, darling," she said, touching her glass to his in a silent toast.

As Lucas and Elena approached, Gabriel turned to face them, his eyes narrowing slightly as he assessed the newcomers. Lucas extended a hand, his grip firm and confident.

"Mr. Sandoval, it's a pleasure to meet you. I'm Lucas Grant, and this is my wife, Elena. We're very interested in oceanfront properties, and we've heard you're the man to talk to."

Gabriel's eyes flicked between them. "The pleasure is mine, Mr. Grant. And please, call me Gabriel." He turned to Elena, taking her hand gently. "Mrs. Grant, it's a delight to meet you."

Elena smiled warmly. "Thank you, Gabriel. We've heard wonderful things about your properties and are eager to learn more."

Gabriel's lips curved into a charming smile. "I'm always happy to talk about my properties. What kind of oceanfront estate are you looking for?"

"We're looking for something private and secluded," Lucas said. "A place where we can escape from the hustle and bustle of the city and enjoy the tranquility of the ocean."

Gabriel nodded. "I have just the place in mind. Why don't we step outside and talk more about it?"

"We'd love that. It would be an honor to see your work firsthand," Lucas said.

Gabriel gestured for them to follow him, leading them toward a private exit that opened onto a path winding through the golf course.

"The golf course is one of the finest on the coast," Gabriel said, his voice carrying a hint of pride. "Designed to challenge even the most seasoned players while offering breathtaking views of the ocean."

The sound of waves grew louder as they approached the shoreline. The path opened up to a breathtaking villa perched on a cliff overlooking the sea.

"This villa is one of our latest projects. We designed it to offer the ultimate in luxury and comfort."

When they stepped inside, Lucas and Elena were struck by the villa's airy, open design. The floor-to-ceiling windows framed panoramic views of the ocean, flooding the space with natural light.

"The way the light fills the space, and the sound of the ocean… it's perfect," Elena said.

Lucas nodded in agreement. "This is exactly what we've been looking for."

Gabriel smiled. "I'm thrilled to hear that. We take great pride in creating homes that not only meet but exceed our clients' expectations."

As they reached the balcony, Gabriel opened the sliding glass doors, revealing a breathtaking view of the ocean. The balcony was spacious, with comfortable seating arranged to take full advantage of the stunning vista.

"This is my favorite part of the villa," Gabriel said, gesturing to the view. "There's nothing quite like watching the sunset over the ocean from here."

Elena stepped out onto the balcony, her eyes widening as she took in the view. The sun was beginning its descent toward the horizon. The waves sparkled in the fading light, creating a mesmerizing, almost magical scene.

"It's incredible," she said softly. "I can see why this is your favorite spot. In our busy life, we rarely get a moment of quiet."

"Busy life can be all-consuming. But one must find balance, don't you agree?" Gabriel mused.

"Balance and trustworthy associates," Lucas said. "You must've had quite a few of those to reach where you are today."

"Trust is the foundation of all successful ventures. Without it, even the mightiest empires crumble," Gabriel said.

Elena cut in, "Speaking of empires, there's a rumor going around about a mysterious figure running the show lately in Miami. Have you heard of The Phantom?"

Gabriel's laugh was rich. "Myths and legends. Miami loves its stories. There's always someone willing to take credit for another's hard work."

"Of course." Elena smiled. "Just idle gossip at cocktail parties."

"Indeed. Now, if you'll excuse me, I must attend to my other guests." Gabriel inclined his head politely and left.

"Strike out?" Lucas muttered as they watched him leave.

"Looks like it," Elena sighed. "Everyone's playing their part perfectly. Too perfectly. Let's circle back toward the exit."

They meandered, pausing only to share pleasantries.

"I enjoy this afternoon," Lucas muttered once they were out of earshot.

"That's only because I'm by your side," Elena replied, her gaze warm.

"Maybe we should do more undercover assignments," Lucas whispered as they neared the car.

"Never thought I'd have this much fun playing the high-roller," Elena said as she surveyed the grandeur of the golf course one last time.

"So, does that mean you'll finally go out with me?" Lucas teased with a wink.

Elena leaned in and whispered back with a smirk, "I don't date cops, detective."

"You've broken my heart," Lucas exclaimed dramatically.

"How is Ava doing?"

"Ava is thriving and your strategy is working."

"What strategy?" Elena asked.

"Every time I ask you out, you ask about Ava."

Lucas helped Elena into the passenger seat before sliding behind the wheel. As they pulled away from the curb, Lucas glanced in the rearview mirror, assuring that no prying eyes followed.

"Back to the headquarters?" Elena asked, shedding the persona with relief.

"We will return the car and get back to the headquarters."

Chapter 14

Elena's heart raced as she climbed the narrow staircase leading to Miguel's apartment. She had been planning this surprise for days, a well-deserved celebration of his latest academic achievements. The old building was dimly lit, the paint peeling from the walls. She reached his door, took a deep breath, and knocked. When there was no answer, she fished out the spare key Miguel had given her and let herself in.

The apartment was cluttered, a far cry from the immaculate space it used to be. The blinds were drawn, casting the room in a murky twilight. Empty bottles and discarded takeout containers littered the floor, and the air was thick with the stale odor of sweat and smoke. Her heart sank as she took in the scene.

"Miguel?" she called softly.

She found him on the couch, slumped over and barely responsive. Miguel was a shadow of the man she remembered. His normally vibrant brown eyes were glazed and unfocused, pupils dilated to unnatural sizes, a telltale sign of intoxication. His skin was pale and clammy, a sheen of sweat covering his forehead. His dark hair, usually neat, was disheveled and matted.

He was dressed in a wrinkled T-shirt and jeans that looked like they hadn't been washed in days. His hands trembled, fingers twitching involuntarily. The track marks on his arms were fresh, angry red punctures that stood out against his skin. His breathing was shallow and erratic, each breath a struggle.

Elena's eyes filled with tears as she knelt beside him. "Miguel, it's me, Elena." She placed a hand on his arm. "Can you hear me?"

Miguel's head lolled to the side, and he blinked slowly, struggling to focus on her. "Elena?" he mumbled. "What are you doing here?"

Scattered around him, like a macabre collection, were small bags of drugs, their contents glinting ominously in the sparse light. A few bags were labeled with a crude "E" written in black marker.

"Miguel, what is this? Are you using Eclipse?" Elena asked.

Miguel blinked slowly. "Elena..." he murmured, his words trailing off.

"Talk to me, Miguel!" Elena took a step forward, her detective instincts melding with sisterly concern. "Why are you involved with Eclipse? Do you have any idea how dangerous this is?"

She crouched down to his level, searching the depths of his clouded eyes for a flicker of the brother she knew—a young man full of potential, not the lost soul who stared back at her now.

"Come on, Miguel. You're smarter than this. Why are you doing this to yourself?"

His mouth opened, but no coherent explanation came forth.

"Talk to me," Elena urged.

Miguel's eyes, reddened and brimming with unshed tears, met hers. "It's... it was the crypto, Elena," he confessed, his voice a hoarse rasp. "I invested everything, and it just... plummeted. Overnight."

"Dammit, Miguel." Elena's heart sank; she'd heard about the crash, but never imagined Miguel would be caught up in it.

"I owe them money," he continued, a tremor in his voice betraying his fear. "A lot of it. And they... they offered a way out. Selling Eclipse on campuses. I thought it'd be quick, just until I got back on my feet."

"Quick?" Elena's voice rose. "You think dealing drugs is a 'quick' fix? This isn't some game, Miguel. You're in deep with these people now."

He winced, as if her words were physical blows. "I know, I know it was stupid. But I felt like I had no choice."

"Of course, you had a choice!" Elena shot back. "Do you even understand what you've gotten into?"

Miguel nodded slowly, a shiver coursing through him. "I do now."

"Then you need to get out," Elena said firmly. "You can't play around with this kind of fire, Miguel. These drug rings are ruthless—they are just using you. We need to act before it's too late. Before you're in any deeper."

Her brother looked so small then, so vulnerable. It pained Elena to see him this way, but she couldn't let her emotions overrule the gravity of the situation.

"You'll leave this behind. If you don't, I'll have no choice but to arrest you right here and take you to the station myself," she warned, reaching out to grasp his cold hand.

The silence that fell between them was heavy. Miguel's nod was almost imperceptible, but Elena caught it.

"Listen to me, Miguel. The first thing you're going to do is cut contact with anyone from that ring. No calls, no messages," Elena instructed.

"Okay," he whispered.

"Next, you and I will go talk to Lucas to see what is the best option for you going forward. Maybe you can help us topple the drug ring so that any charges against you can be dropped."

Miguel nodded slowly.

"Write down any information you know about the drug ring—names, schedules, drop points, anything that can help us predict their moves."

"Okay, I will do that. Will I go to prison?" Miguel asked.

"I don't know. Helping the police is your best option right now."

"Elena... I..." His throat bobbed as he swallowed hard.

"Shhh," she soothed, wrapping her arms around him. "I'm here now. We're going to get through this together."

For a long moment, they remained locked in the embrace.

"Elena... I'm so sorry. For all of this," Miguel's voice cracked.

"I know, Miguel. But sorry isn't enough. You have to make this right. And it starts now."

Chapter 15

The low hum of computer fans and the gentle tapping of keys filled the Narcotics Unit office. The bluish glow from the monitors illuminated everything in sight. Baxter sat at the main workstation, his fingers moving rapidly across the keyboard as he worked through a maze of databases and advanced search algorithms. Lucas stood behind him, shifting his weight back and forth between his feet.

"Any luck yet?" Lucas asked.

"Patience," Baxter murmured, his eyes fixed on the screen. "Give me a minute, Lucas. This AI system is sifting through a lot of data. Vincent's not exactly an uncommon name. It's like finding a needle in a digital haystack."

Lucas sighed, and he watched Baxter's screen filled with lines of code, facial recognition scans, and cross-references from various law enforcement databases.

After what felt like an eternity, Baxter's eyes widened. "Got something!" he exclaimed, his fingers pausing on the keyboard. "Vincent Rogers. He's got a record. Multiple felonies, mostly related to drug trafficking and armed robbery. AI flagged him in connection to the warehouse that you raided."

Lucas leaned in closer, his eyes narrowing as he scanned the information on the screen. "Rogers... and his connections?"

Baxter nodded, his fingers resuming their dance across the keys. "Give me a moment to dig deeper." The AI continued to process, compiling a detailed dossier on Vincent Rogers. Images, addresses, known associates, and criminal affiliations flashed across the screen.

"Vincent Rogers has been in and out of that warehouse for years, running operations right under our noses," Baxter said.

"Great job, Baxter. Send me his home address, phone number, and names of anyone he associates with," Lucas said, his excitement growing. He reached for his phone tucked in his belt. "Elena, call the team. Briefing in ten."

As officers began to trickle into the briefing room, Lucas paced at the head of the table. The walls were lined with maps and photographs. Elena stood beside him, her sharp eyes scanning over the equipment laid out on the table: bulletproof vests, radios, and an array of weaponry.

"Listen up," Lucas said. "We hit Vincent Rogers' place this afternoon. Full gear. We're aiming to bring him in and shake down any info on The Phantom."

"Expect resistance?" one officer asked, checking the clip in his sidearm.

"Always do," Lucas replied. "This is bigger than just another bust."

"Let's go over entry points," Elena said, pointing to the blueprints of Vincent's house. She detailed the plan, her finger tracing the path they would take.

"Remember," Lucas added, "Vincent is our key to dismantling this whole damn thing. We must not let him escape. Alright, let's roll."

***

The convoy of police cars rolled to a stop a few houses down from their target, Vincent Rogers' residence in suburban Miami. It was 3:00 PM, and the late afternoon sun cast long shadows across the tree-lined street. The neighborhood was a picture of suburban tranquility, with well-kept lawns and the occasional sound of children playing in the distance.

Vincent's house stood out as more fortified than the others. It was a two-story structure with a stucco exterior painted a pale beige, accented with dark brown shutters and a matching front door. The high, dense hedges surrounding the property suggested a desire for privacy.

Lucas, Elena, and their team gathered behind the cover of a large oak tree. Lucas adjusted his bulletproof vest, his eyes scanning the house for any signs of movement. "Alright, team, you know the drill. We go in fast and hard. No mistakes."

Elena nodded. "Remember, Vincent is likely armed and dangerous. Stay alert."

The team moved silently, taking their positions around the house. Lucas, Elena, and two other officers approached the front door, while Tom and Baxter circled to the back. The rear of the house had a small patio area with a barbecue grill and a few lounge chairs. French doors with heavy curtains offered entry into the house.

"Tom, you good?" Lucas whispered into his comms.

"Clear on my end." Tom's voice crackled through the earpieces, "No movements at the back."

Lucas signaled to Elena, who nodded and positioned herself on the opposite side of the doors.

"Breaching in three... two... one..." With a swift motion, Lucas motioned for the battering ram to be brought forward. An officer swung the battering ram with force, splintering the door frame and sending the doors crashing open.

"Police! Hands in the air!" Lucas shouted as they stormed inside.

The living room was spacious, with leather furniture and a large flat-screen TV mounted on the wall. The kitchen had stainless steel appliances and granite countertops, clean and organized.

The team moved quickly through the ground floor, clearing each room.

"Clear downstairs," Elena reported.

"Upstairs, move!" Lucas commanded, leading the charge up the stairs. The team fanned out, methodically checking each bedroom and bathroom. The master bedroom door was slightly ajar, and Lucas motioned for the team to proceed with caution.

Inside the master bedroom, a king-sized bed with a tufted headboard dominated the room, flanked by matching nightstands. Heavy drapes covered the windows, blocking out most of the sunlight. A large walk-in closet stood to one side, and the door was slightly open.

Lucas signaled to an officer to check the closet while he and Elena approached the ensuite bathroom. The bathroom door was closed, and Lucas pressed his ear to it, listening for any signs of movement. He nodded to Elena, and they prepared to breach.

In a swift move, Lucas kicked the door open, his weapon raised. The bathroom was empty, but the window was slightly open, the curtains billowing in the breeze. Elena checked the window. "He might have escaped through here," she said, frustration creeping into her voice.

"Damm it," Lucas muttered. He turned to the team. "Let's canvas the neighborhood. Someone must've seen something. And get forensics in here; they might find something we missed."

"Got it," Elena said, following him out. "I'll put out an APB on Vincent. If he's still in Miami, we'll find him."

"Vincent left in a hurry. He can't have gone too far," Lucas said.

Chapter 16

The setting sun bathed the idyllic Coral Gables neighborhood in a golden light. Lucas parked his Ford Explorer on the street, a sense of relief washing over him. His townhouse, a charming Mediterranean-style home, stood proudly among its neighbors. The exterior was painted a soft beige, with terracotta roof tiles and arched windows framed by vibrant bougainvillea. A small lawn led up to the front porch, where a pair of wrought-iron chairs invited relaxation.

Lucas walked toward the front door, enjoying the scent of jasmine from a nearby garden. He reached into his pocket for keys, the familiar jingle a comforting sound as he approached the steps.

Suddenly, the sharp, staccato sound of gunfire erupted, bullets whizzing past him, splintering the wooden porch railing and shattering the front window. Instinctively, Lucas dove for cover behind the large ceramic planter on the edge of the porch, his heart pounding. His mind raced as he assessed the situation. This wasn't a random act of violence—it was an ambush. The Phantom's crew had found him.

Peering cautiously from behind the planter, Lucas caught a glimpse of his attackers. Three men, dressed in dark clothing and masks, were positioned behind a black SUV parked across the street. Their weapons were trained on him, and they were moving with the precision of trained operatives. He could see the muzzle flashes as they fired, the air around him filled with the acrid smell of gunpowder.

"Detective! You can't beat The Phantom!" a voice taunted.

"Watch me," Lucas muttered. He drew his Glock, his hands steady despite the adrenaline coursing through his veins.

He waited for a brief lull in the gunfire, then sprang into action. He rolled to his left, firing a few shots in the direction of the SUV as he moved toward the side of the house.

"Come out, detective! It'll be quick!" another voice called, closer this time. They were flanking him.

"Like hell," Lucas spat back, rolling across the asphalt to take cover behind a trashcan. Splinters flew as a bullet obliterated the spot where he had just been.

"Give it up, Grant!" The words were punctuated by another round of gunfire.

Lucas popped out from his cover, firing three precise shots at the attackers. A yelp told him he'd hit something—someone.

"Police's on the way," he said loudly, hoping to unnerve them. The response was a hailstorm of bullets, chipping away at his refuge.

"Police won't find anything but your body! Are you looking for us? We are here!"

"Talk is cheap," Lucas retorted. He dashed to a new hiding spot, a low wall by his neighbor's yard. Bullets followed, nipping at his heels.

"Got you now, Grant!" The voice was almost gleeful.

"Think again!" Lucas shot back. His return fire was swift, a bullet grazing his left arm in the process—a sharp burn, but nothing to slow him down.

"Argh!" came a pained shout, then the sound of someone retreating.

Using the shadows as cover, Lucas slipped through the narrow space between houses, clutching his wounded arm.

Sirens wailed in the distance, growing louder. Help was coming now. Lucas allowed himself a shallow breath of relief. He checked his left arm—blood, but he'd live.

"Close call, Lucas," he whispered to himself, leaning against the bricks of an alley. His pulse began to settle, the night air helping to clear the fog of battle. The Phantom's crew had left.

Lucas's fingers, slick with blood, fumbled for his phone.

"This is Detective Grant. I was ambushed and need immediate assistance at my residence. Send a paramedic and a tactical unit."

He tapped Elena's contact on his phone.

"Lucas," she answered immediately.

"Watch out," Lucas cautioned. "The Phantom's crew ambushed me outside my place."

"Lucas! Are you hurt?" Elena's voice was laced with worry and urgency. "I'm coming over right now."

"It's not too bad." Lucas leaned against the wall, feeling a sharp pain in his arm. "A squad car is already here, and a paramedic should be arriving soon."

Half an hour later, Elena arrived and quickly took in the scene.

"How are you holding up, Lucas?" Her voice shook slightly.

"I'll be okay," Lucas reassured her as he continued to receive treatment from the paramedic.

"The bullet just grazed you," the paramedic remarked while securing a tight bandage around the wound. "You're lucky."

"Or they were terrible shots," Lucas quipped, testing his fingers once the bandage was in place. "Thanks for your help."

"Did you get a look at their faces?" Elena asked, stepping closer. She gazed into his eyes and embraced him tightly.

"They were wearing masks. A black SUV parked across the street and at least three shooters came after me," Lucas replied through clenched teeth as the pain throbbed in his arm. "Probably ex-military."

"You need to rest and let me handle this," Elena said firmly.

Lucas nodded in agreement. Elena turned on her heel and began directing the patrolmen to gather bullet casings for ballistic analysis.

Chapter 17

The fluorescent lights hummed in a steady rhythm, illuminating the rows of screens in the Narcotics Unit office. Baxter's fingers flew across the keyboard as he scanned the various windows displaying data on his monitors.

"Got something," Baxter announced, without turning from the screen.

Lucas leaned in over Baxter's shoulder, his muscular frame tensing as he focused on the grainy CCD footage that had been pulled up. There, in the corner of the screen, was Vincent Rogers, unmistakable even in the low-resolution capture, slipping into a motel room.

"How recent is this?" Lucas asked.

"Timestamp says sixty-five minutes ago."

"Alright, let's roll out," Lucas commanded, clapping Baxter on the back with a firm hand.

***

The sun cast stark shadows over the deserted streets of Overtown in Miami, as Lucas, Elena, and their team arrived at the isolated motel. The small, run-down establishment was a relic from a bygone era, with a faded sign that read "Sunset Inn."

The parking lot was mostly empty, with weeds sprouting through cracks in the worn asphalt and glimmering shards of broken glass scattered around like sinister stars. Made of weathered wood, the two-story structure showed its age with chipped edges. The windows were dirty and some were boarded up, while others had tattered curtains fluttering through shattered panes.

Lucas stepped out of the car, the oppressive heat and humidity hitting him like a wall.

"A good place to hide out," Elena muttered, glancing around at the desolate surroundings.

"Room 12, end of the walkway," Lucas whispered into his earpiece, gripping his Glock. The rest of the team acknowledged with barely audible clicks.

"Keep it tight," he reminded them.

Lucas took point, his piercing gaze scanning for any sign of movement behind the tattered curtains of Room 12.

"Ready?" he mouthed to the team, receiving a series of subtle nods in response.

They positioned themselves strategically, forming a semi-circle around the door. Lucas raised his hand, three fingers up, then two, then one, and...

"Police! Open up!" Lucas shouted, pounding on the door of Room 12. When there was no response, he signaled for the battering ram. The door splintered open with a deafening crash, and the team surged inside, weapons at the ready.

The room was a chaotic mess of discarded clothing, empty food containers, and scattered belongings. The air was thick with the scent of sweat and cigarette smoke. Lucas's eyes scanned the room, but it was empty. He heard a faint rustling from the bathroom and motioned for Elena to cover him.

"Vincent Rogers, Miami PD! Come out with your hands up!" Lucas commanded, moving toward the closed bathroom door.

Silence.

"Last chance before we come in!" he warned, tightening his grip on his weapon.

No response.

Lucas kicked the door open and stepped inside. Vincent burst out from behind the door, his eyes wide. Lucas barely had time to react before a fist slammed into his jaw, sending a jolt of pain radiating through his skull. Vincent was a tall, muscular man with a rugged face. His dark hair was greasy and disheveled, and a scruffy beard covered his jaw. His eyes were filled with a mix of defiance and fear. Tattoos snaked up his arms, visible beneath his grimy T-shirt.

"Lucas!" Elena's voice was a distant echo as he grappled with Vincent, both men crashing into the flimsy shower curtain, tearing it from the rings.

"Get off me!" Vincent snarled, throwing another punch. Lucas dodged, feeling the rush of adrenaline sharpening his reflexes. He countered with a blow to Vincent's midsection.

"Fuck—" Vincent gasped, reeling from the impact.

Elena and two other officers barreled into the cramped bathroom. Tiles clattered to the floor like fallen soldiers as Lucas and Vincent continued their ferocious struggle.

Lucas winced as Vincent's elbow caught his bandaged arm, causing a sharp ache to radiate through his left shoulder.

"Got him!" One officer lunged forward, grabbing Vincent's flailing legs.

Elena helped Lucas twist the henchman's arm behind his back, pressing it upwards until the fight drained from Vincent's body.

The handcuffs snapped shut with a loud click. Vincent's body slumped, surrendering to defeat and exhaustion.

"Bastard!" Lucas snarled, his chest heaving as he took a step back. "You're done running."

"You have no idea what you're getting into," Vincent hissed, his breath coming in ragged gasps. "You think you can stop this?"

"We'll find out." Lucas pulled Vincent to his feet. Elena took hold of Vincent's arm and led him out of the bathroom.

"Let's get him out of here," Lucas said.

They escorted Vincent through the tattered remains of the motel room, past the splintered door.

"Watch your head," Elena directed as Vincent was lowered into the back of a police sedan.

"Police station," Lucas instructed the driver before sliding into the seat beside Vincent. Elena took the passenger seat. The engine roared to life, and the vehicle pulled away from the curb.

Chapter 18

The interrogation room at the police station was a space designed to break down the defenses of anyone who entered. The walls were painted gray, devoid of any decoration that might provide comfort or distraction. A metal table occupied the center of the room, flanked by two hard plastic chairs on one side and a metal chair on the other.

A large, one-way mirror dominated one wall, allowing observers to watch the proceedings from the adjoining room. The fluorescent lights above were unforgiving. The air was cool, carrying the faint scent of disinfectant.

Lucas sat across from Vincent, who was handcuffed to the metal chair. He leaned forward, his hands resting on the table, his eyes locked onto Vincent's. "You know why you're here, Vincent. We've got you on charges ranging from drug trafficking to murder. The sooner you start talking, the better it'll be for you."

Elena leaned against the wall, arms crossed. Her gaze was fixed on Vincent.

Vincent scoffed. "You think you scare me? I've dealt with worse than you."

"This isn't a game, Vincent. The more you cooperate, the more we can help you. But if you keep stonewalling, things will only get worse," Elena said.

Vincent shifted in his chair, the handcuffs clinking against the metal. "You've got nothing on me. You're wasting your time."

Lucas's gaze didn't waver. "We have enough evidence to put you away for a long time. But we're more interested in your associates. If you can provide information on The Phantom and their associates, perhaps we can negotiate a deal."

Vincent's eyes flickered with a moment of uncertainty before hardening again. "I don't know anyone named Phantom. I want a lawyer."

"We already know a lot about you, Vincent. We know you work for The Phantom, and that you've been in and out of that warehouse at 1345 NE 22nd Street. This is your chance to save yourself," Elena said.

Vincent's jaw clenched, a muscle ticking in his cheek. "You don't know anything."

"Listen to me, Vincent." Lucas slammed his fist on the cold metal table and leaned in closer. "You've been caught and are no longer useful to The Phantom. You're a small fish in a big pond. The Phantom won't hesitate to cut you loose. He's probably already ordered for you to be eliminated so you can't talk. Give us something we can use, and we can protect you. Keep playing tough, and you're on your own."

Vincent's eyes darted between Lucas and Elena. His fingers tapped a staccato rhythm on the table, betraying his anxiety.

"Vincent, tell us about Sofia," Lucas said, sliding a photograph across the table. The glossy image displayed the lifeless body of Sofia Morales, her head missing and her hands tightly bound with rough rope.

"Never seen her before," Vincent muttered.

"Cut the crap, Vincent. We've got witnesses, surveillance... your prints are all over her nightclub," Elena interjected sharply, her dark eyes flashing. "You were there the night she was killed."

"Didn't kill her," Vincent insisted, but sweat beaded on his forehead.

"Then tell us who did. Who gave the order?" Lucas leaned in closer, his muscular frame imposing even seated. "You're looking at electrocution, Vincent. Help us, and maybe we can help you."

"I can't..." he started, voice barely above a whisper.

"Can't or won't?" Elena challenged. "We can make a deal, Vincent. Witness protection, a reduced sentence—these are on the table if you cooperate. Think about it. Do you really want to take the fall for everything? Or do you want a way out?"

Vincent's shoulders slumped slightly, the fight beginning to drain from him. He glanced at the one-way mirror, as if searching for an unseen ally, but found none.

"Alright," he said, his voice barely above a whisper. "I'll talk. But I want guarantees."

Lucas nodded. "You cooperate, and we'll make sure you get a fair deal. Now, tell us everything you know about The Phantom."

"Gabriel Sandoval is The Phantom."

"Gabriel Sandoval?" Lucas feigned surprise. "The real estate mogul? What's he got to do with this?"

"Everything," Vincent blurted out, his composure shattering like glass. "He's not just some businessman. He's The Phantom."

A knowing look passed between Lucas and Elena, the significance of what was just revealed sinking in. They had suspected as much, but hearing it confirmed from Vincent's lips was another matter entirely.

"Tell us more about Gabriel Sandoval—about The Phantom," Lucas pressed.

"Order came down. It was meant to be a warning for Sofia—to scare her off. Things went south..." Vincent trailed off, shaking his head.

"Who gave the order, Vincent?" Elena's voice sliced through the tension.

"Rafael," he admitted. "Rafael Sandoval."

"His son," Lucas murmured, the puzzle pieces clicking into place.

"Is Rafael managing the operations?" Elena asked, stepping forward.

"Look, I've said enough already," Vincent said, clamping up. "My life's as good as over."

"Work with us, Vincent. We can offer protection," Lucas said, his tone softening. "You need to trust us."

Vincent's eyes flickered to the mirrored glass, then back to the detectives.

"Alright, but you gotta promise me—"

"We'll keep you safe, Vincent," Elena assured him.

Lucas leaned in across the cold metal table. "Rafael, what part does he play in all of this?"

"Everything," Vincent whispered. "He oversees it all... The manufacture, distribution, the cash flow... He gives orders to seize territories from the Scales Cartel."

"Where do you manufacture Eclipse, the drug?" Elena probed.

"Gabriel's mansion," Vincent murmured, looking defeated. "There's a basement—no, more like a fortress under the house. That's where they make it all happen. That's the heart."

"Can you be more specific?" Lucas asked. "We need details."

"Gabriel has an oceanfront mansion at the southside of the city. The east wing of the mansion... hidden door behind the wine cellar. It leads down to the labs, and the storage rooms. They control everything from there."

"Good," Lucas said, nodding.

"Lucas," Elena spoke up once they were alone. "This is it. If Rafael is truly running the show as Vincent says, taking down the manufacturing site could dismantle The Phantom's entire operation."

"Agreed. We hit them hard and fast. Surprise is our best weapon."

"It's a big operation. We need to get DEA involved," Elena added.

"I'll talk to the Captain," Lucas said.

***

Lucas strode into Captain Rodriguez's office, causing her to look up from her desk.

"Captain," Lucas began, "We have testimony from Vincent Rogers stating that Gabriel Sandoval is The Phantom. We've also located his manufacturing site. We plan to launch a raid on the location."

"Well done." Rodriguez stood up from her chair. "Where exactly is this manufacturing site?"

"It's in the underground level of a mansion by the oceanfront. We need to move quickly."

"I will inform Agent Jackson," Rodriguez said, her hand already reaching for the landline. Elena slipped into the room behind Lucas.

"Agent Jackson," Rodriguez barked into the receiver moments later. "Rodriguez. We've got a go on Gabriel Sandoval's manufacturing site. You in?"

"I've heard the good news! Congratulations to Lucas and his team. Count us in," came the voice of Calvin Jackson over the speakerphone. "My team is ready to mobilize."

"Resources?" Elena interjected, stepping forward. "We'll need tactical support, surveillance, the works."

"Surveillance drones are at your disposal, and I can secure a chopper for aerial support," Calvin offered. "How soon can you move?"

Lucas glanced at his watch before speaking. "We're going to strike them tomorrow at noon." He added, "Since it's an ocean-front location, we'll also need a patrol boat on standby in case they try to flee by sea."

"Then we don't have a second to waste," Rodriguez snapped. "I'll get SWAT teams on standby. We can't afford any leaks. Lockdown on all communications starts now. Only encrypted channels from here on out."

"Understood," Lucas and Elena responded in unison.

"Check your gear, then meet in Briefing Room One at 0900 tomorrow," Rodriguez instructed.

Chapter 19

The late morning sun bathed the oceanfront mansion in a golden glow. The sprawling estate overlooked the azure expanse of the Atlantic Ocean, its white stucco walls and red-tiled roof a stark contrast against the lush greenery that surrounded it. Tall palm trees swayed gently in the breeze, adding to the serene façade that belied the sinister activities hidden within.

A grand stone staircase led up to the imposing front entrance, flanked by statues of mythological figures that stood as silent sentinels. The driveway was lined with trimmed hedges and vibrant flowerbeds, and a large, ornate fountain dominated the circular drive, its water sparkling in the sunlight.

Lucas, Elena, and their team parked their vehicles a short distance away, and they quickly disembarked.

Lucas adjusted his tactical vest, his eyes narrowing as he scanned the sprawling estate. Beside him, Elena checked her weapon one last time.

"Everyone ready?" Lucas asked, his voice low.

A chorus of affirmatives followed. DEA agent Calvin Jackson gave a curt nod to his team.

"Remember, these guys are heavily armed and dangerous," Calvin reminded. "Stay sharp and watch each other's backs."

At noon on the dot, they arrived at the gate, where two guards stood watch. The guards were dressed in dark suits and had sunglasses perched atop their noses. Each of them carried a semi-automatic pistol strapped to their side, standing at attention.

The team split into two groups, with Lucas and Elena taking the lead. They communicated through hand signals, coordinating their approach.

Lucas spotted a narrow path through the dense hedges that offered cover as they advanced toward the guards. He motioned for Elena to follow. They crouched low, moving silently through the greenery until they were just a few feet from the guards. The sound of the ocean waves and the rustling of palm fronds helped mask their approach.

At Lucas's signal, they sprang into action. Lucas lunged toward the guard on the left, his movements swift and fluid. In one motion, he grabbed the guard's wrist, twisting it sharply to disarm him. The guard's pistol clattered to the ground as Lucas delivered a precise strike to his solar plexus, knocking the wind out of him. Before the guard could react, Lucas spun him around, locking his arm behind his back and pressing him against the gate.

Simultaneously, Elena engaged the guard on the right. She moved with the speed of a trained fighter, closing the distance in an instant. She feinted a punch to the guard's face, causing him to instinctively raise his arms in defense. Using the opening, Elena stepped in and delivered a powerful knee to his abdomen, followed by an elbow strike to his jaw. The guard stumbled, dazed by the rapid assault.

As the guard tried to recover, Elena swept his legs out from under him with a low kick, sending him sprawling to the ground. She quickly knelt beside him, applying pressure to a nerve point on his neck to incapacitate him while she stripped him of his weapon. The guard groaned, unable to resist as she secured his hands with a pair of zip ties.

With both guards disarmed and subdued in a matter of seconds, Lucas and Elena exchanged a quick nod. Lucas retrieved the fallen pistol from the ground, while Elena scanned the area for any additional threats.

"Clear," Elena whispered.

"Secure them," Lucas instructed, indicating the guards. The rest of the team moved in, quickly binding the guards' hands and gagging them to prevent any noise. They stashed the subdued guards behind the dense hedges, hidden from view.

Lucas and Elena took a moment to catch their breath. Lucas glanced at his watch, noting the time. "Let's move." The team moved forward, quickly closing the distance to the mansion's front door. The grand entrance loomed before them, its heavy wooden doors carved with intricate designs.

Elena signaled the breaching team, who positioned themselves at the door. With a nod from Lucas, the battering ram was swung into action, smashing the doors open with a resounding crash. The team surged inside, weapons drawn.

The interior of the mansion was as opulent as the exterior. The foyer was a vast, marble-floored space with a grand chandelier hanging from the high ceiling. A sweeping staircase with an ornate wrought-iron railing curved up to the second floor, and expensive artwork adorned the walls.

For a brief moment, there was silence. Then, all hell broke loose.

A hail of bullets erupted from inside the mansion. Lucas dove to the side, taking cover behind a marble column as bullets whizzed past him, chipping away at the polished stone. Elena returned fire, as she aimed at the shadowy figures within.

"Take cover!" Calvin's voice boomed over the chaos, his team fanning out to find cover.

The air was thick with the smell of gunpowder and the acrid scent of smoke. Shouts and screams mingled with the relentless barrage of gunfire. Lucas peeked out from behind the column, his eyes locking onto a figure silhouetted in the doorway.

"Elena, on your right!" he shouted, firing off a burst of bullets.

Elena pivoted. Her shots found their mark, and one of the assailants crumpled to the floor. But more were coming, pouring out of the mansion like a swarm of angry bees.

"We need to push forward!" Calvin yelled.

Lucas nodded, signaling to his team to advance. They moved as one, a wall of firepower. Inch by inch, they gained ground, their progress marked by the bodies of the fallen Phantom crews.

"Keep moving!" Elena urged.

The mansion's basement door loomed ahead, its surface cold. Lucas knelt by the metal door, his lock-picking tool already in hand. With practiced precision, he manipulated the tool, the lock surrendering with a quiet click. He pushed the door open and hurried down the stairs with Elena.

The basement was vast, illuminated by a harsh array of fluorescent lights. The industrial hum of machinery filled the air, mingling with the acrid smell of chemicals. The facility was a labyrinth of stainless steel tables, each covered with glass beakers, Bunsen burners, and a myriad of chemical containers.

Over twenty workers in lab coats and safety goggles froze as Lucas and Elena burst in. Their expressions ranged from shock to terror, hands slowly rising in a sign of surrender.

"Hands up! Don't move!" Elena shouted.

The workers obeyed, their eyes wide with fear. Lucas quickly scanned the room, taking in the scale of the operation. In the center, a massive industrial mixer churned a thick, white substance with relentless efficiency. Stacks of sealed barrels and crates filled with finished products lined the walls, each marked with hazardous symbols and cryptic labels.

Against one wall, a series of computers and monitoring equipment displayed streams of data and surveillance feeds. The room was a high-tech nerve center, meticulously designed for efficiency and secrecy. Lucas noted the complex chemical formulas and production statistics flashing across the screens, a testament to the sophistication of The Phantoms' drug manufacturing empire.

"Keep your hands where we can see them!" Lucas barked, moving toward the nearest worker. "Anyone tries anything, you'll regret it."

Elena approached a table stacked with ledgers and notebooks, her eyes scanning the handwritten notes and financial records.

"Lucas, look at this," she said, holding up a ledger. "These records detail everything—contacts, distribution routes, supply chains. This is the jackpot."

Lucas took the ledger, quickly flipping through its pages. "Let's secure the rest of the evidence and get these people out of here."

He turned to address the workers. "You're all under arrest for your involvement in this operation. Cooperate, and we'll sort this out. Resist, and you'll face the consequences."

A murmur of fear and resignation rippled through the crowd. As the first officers descended the stairs, Lucas handed over the ledgers and evidence. " Secure this evidence," he commanded. "Take all of these individuals into custody."

Lucas scanned the room, looking for the one person they needed most—Rafael, Gabriel's son and the mastermind behind the drug manufacturing facility.

"Elena, have you seen Rafael?" Lucas called out.

"No, not yet," Elena replied, glancing around. "He has to be here somewhere."

Suddenly, the radio crackled to life. "Lucas, this is Calvin. I've got eyes on Rafael. He's at the docking area in the rear of the mansion, trying to escape on a speedboat."

Lucas's heart raced. "Copy that, Calvin. We're on our way."

Lucas and Elena sprinted through the mansion, burst through a side door, and emerged into the bright sunlight. The sprawling estate gave way to a private docking area. In the distance, they saw Rafael clambered onto a sleek speedboat.

"He's not getting away," Lucas muttered.

Nearby, a police patrol boat bobbed gently in the water. The officers on board, alerted by the commotion, waved them over.

"We need your boat!" Elena shouted.

"Get on, quick!" one of the officers replied, helping them aboard.

As soon as Lucas and Elena were on the patrol boat, an officer gunned the engine, and they sped off in pursuit of Rafael. The patrol boat roared to life, skimming across the water with terrifying speed.

Rafael glanced back, his eyes widening as he saw the patrol boat gaining on him. He was in his mid-30s, tall and lean, with an air of arrogance that matched his ruthless reputation. His dark hair, slicked back from his forehead, gleamed in the sunlight. Rafael navigated the black speedboat, its powerful engine roaring as it cut through the water.

"Stay on him!" Lucas yelled, gripping the side of the patrol boat. The patrol boat's engine roared, matching the speed of Rafael's vessel.

Rafael's speedboat darted and weaved, trying to shake them, but the patrol boat stayed close, matching every maneuver. Elena crouched beside Lucas and readied her weapon, her eyes fixed on their target.

"Calvin, we're in pursuit," Lucas said into his radio.

"Understood," Calvin's voice crackled back. "Be careful. Rafael is desperate."

Rafael's boat veered sharply to the left, heading toward a narrow channel flanked by rocky outcroppings. The patrol boat followed, navigating the treacherous waters. Lucas felt a surge of adrenaline as they closed the gap between the boats.

"Just a little closer," Lucas said.

Rafael glanced over his shoulder and pushed the throttle forward, coaxing every ounce of speed from the engine. The speedboat leaped forward, its hull skimming the surface of the water, sending spray flying in all directions.

As the boats drew closer, Elena stood, her weapon aimed at Rafael's boat. "Rafael! Stop the boat! There's nowhere to run!" she shouted.

Rafael glanced back again, his expression a mix of fear and defiance. Instead of slowing down, he pushed the throttle harder.

"Damn it, he's not stopping," Lucas muttered.

The channel grew narrower, the rocks on either side looming ominously. Lucas knew they had to act fast before Rafael tried something reckless. He signaled to the officer at the helm of the patrol boat, who nodded in understanding.

"We're going to pull alongside him," the officer shouted. "Get ready to board!"

The patrol boat edged closer, the two vessels almost parallel now. Elena kept her weapon trained on Rafael, her finger steady on the trigger. Lucas moved to the edge of the boat, preparing to leap onto Rafael's speedboat.

In a daring move, the patrol boat surged forward, closing the final gap. Lucas leaped from the patrol boat, landing on the deck of Rafael's speedboat.

Rafael spun around, his eyes widening in surprise. He reached for a gun tucked into the waistband of his pants, but Lucas was faster. He tackled Rafael, the force of the impact sending them both crashing to the deck. The gun skittered across the deck, sliding out of reach.

The two men grappled, the boat rocking violently beneath them as it sped across the waves. Rafael fought with the ferocity of a cornered animal, his fists swinging wildly.

With a powerful punch, Lucas sent Rafael sprawling to the deck, his head hitting the metal with a sickening thud.

Rafael lay still, his eyes glazed and unfocused, blood trickling from a cut on his forehead.

Lucas quickly secured Rafael's hands with a pair of handcuffs, pulling him to his feet. "It's over, Rafael. You're not going anywhere."

Elena jumped aboard, her weapon trained on Rafael.

"Got him," Lucas said, breathing heavily.

The patrol boat slowed, the officers moving to help secure Rafael.

"Nice work," Elena said.

"You too," Lucas replied, the adrenaline slowly ebbing away. "Let's get him back."

The patrol boat turned back toward the mansion, the sun beginning to set on a day of hard-won victory. Lucas couldn't help but feel a sense of accomplishment.

Chapter 20

In the interrogation room, Rafael sat at the metal table, his wrists cuffed and his expression unyielding. Lucas and Elena stood on the other side, their eyes locked on the notorious drug lord.

"Rafael," Lucas began. "Let's not waste time. We know you're neck-deep in your father's drug business."

Elena remained silent, her dark eyes studying Rafael's every micro-expression.

"Gabriel Sandoval," Lucas leaned forward, placing his palms flat against the table, the muscles in his forearms tensing like steel cables. "Where is he?"

Rafael leaned back in his chair, a smug smile tugging at the corners of his lips. "You think you've got something on me, don't you? I'm not saying a word without my lawyer present."

"The sooner you start talking, the better it'll be for you. Your lawyer can't protect you from everything," Lucas shot back.

"I suppose we'll find out, won't we? Want to know where my father is? Go check out his house. You can find the address on his driver's license. And I bet you two are the same detectives who were snooping around his private golf course a few days ago. Did you put a down payment on that oceanfront villa yet? Or is it too expensive for your detective salaries? If you let me go, I'll give you a generous discount."

Elena's jaw tightened. "Rafael, this isn't a game."

Rafael shrugged, his eyes glinting with defiance. "I know my rights. Until my lawyer gets here, I'm not saying a word."

Before Lucas could respond, a sudden commotion erupted outside the room. Raised voices and the sound of hurried footsteps echoed through the hallway. The door to the interrogation room burst open, and Tom rushed in, his eyes wide with urgency.

"Lucas, I need to speak with you. Now," Tom said.

Lucas exchanged a puzzled glance with Elena before nodding. "Keep an eye on him," he said to Elena. He followed Tom out into the hallway, the door closing behind them with a click.

Tom led Lucas to a quieter corner, his face etched with worry.

"What's going on, Tom?" Lucas asked.

"It's Vincent Rogers. He's been shot and killed in the holding cell downstairs."

"What? How did this happen?"

"A man posing as a lawyer managed to overpower one of the guards," Tom explained. "He took the guard's gun and shot Vincent before anyone could stop him."

Lucas felt a surge of frustration. Vincent Rogers had been their key witness, the linchpin in their case against Gabriel Sandoval. Now, that critical link was gone.

"Where is the shooter now?" Lucas asked.

"Dead," Tom replied, "taken out by several officers' shots."

"Damn it," Lucas muttered, running a hand through his hair. "Gabriel must have orchestrated this."

Tom nodded. "It's likely."

Lucas took a deep breath, forcing himself to focus. "Alright. We need to lock this area down. No one gets in or out without clearance. We can't afford to lose Rafael."

Tom nodded and turned to leave, but Lucas grabbed his arm. "Tom, keep this quiet for now. Don't tell anyone that Rafael is in the interrogation room. Tell Baxter to come down here. We need extra security."

"Understood," Tom replied. "I'll go get Baxter."

As Tom hurried off, Lucas returned to the interrogation room.

"Elena, can we step outside for a moment?" Lucas gestured to the hallway.

Elena nodded and followed him, pulling the door shut behind her.

"What's going on, Lucas?"

"Vincent's dead," Lucas said curtly. "Someone got to him right under our noses."

"Jesus..." She placed a hand over her mouth.

"Means we've got a mole," Lucas concluded.

"Inside our own house..." Elena murmured.

Lucas knew they were both thinking the same thing: The Phantom had eyes and ears everywhere, and nowhere was safe—not even the heart of Miami PD.

***

Lucas and Elena sat in Captain Rodriguez's office, the tension palpable in the air. Rodriguez sat behind the desk, her fingers steepled as she listened to Lucas and Elena recount the grim details of Vincent Rogers' murder.

"Vincent was our key witness," Lucas said, his voice tight with frustration. "His death dealt a heavy blow to our case against Gabriel Sandoval. It's clear that someone inside the department tipped off Gabriel's crew."

Elena nodded. "We've checked the footage and spoken to the guards, but it's clear there's a mole. We need to act fast before Gabriel's crew can strike again."

Rodriguez's eyes narrowed as she processed the information. "I agree. Vincent is a casualty of our oversight and a reminder that we are compromised from within. We need to move Rafael to a safe house immediately, somewhere secure and off the grid."

She stood and walked over to a large map of the city pinned to the wall. "We have a safe house on the outskirts of the city," she said, pointing to a secluded area near the Everglades. "It's a remote location, well-fortified, and only known to a select few in the department. It's our best chance to keep Rafael secure and alive until we root out the mole. We can move Rafael there tonight."

Lucas leaned forward. "We can't take any chances, Captain. We need the SWAT team to handle the transfer. If Gabriel's crew finds out about this, they'll stop at nothing to rescue Rafael."

Rodriguez nodded. "I'll have the SWAT team ready and briefed. Lucas, you and Elena will oversee the transfer. Coordinate with SWAT and keep me updated. We'll move at 0200 hours to minimize the risk of exposure."

"Yes, Captain," Lucas affirmed.

Elena glanced at Lucas. "We need to make sure every detail is covered. No one outside this room should know who is being moved and where."

Rodriguez turned to face them. "I'll personally oversee the preparations and ensure that the information is tightly controlled. We can't afford any more leaks."

Chapter 21

As the clock inched closer to 0200, the garage of the police station grew darker. The group assembled there waited in silence. Lucas donned a black tactical vest over his navy-blue police uniform, with "POLICE" boldly printed in white letters across his chest. His vest was lined with pouches containing extra magazines, handcuffs, and a radio. His Glock rested on his thigh, accompanied by a combat knife strapped to his vest.

Her dark hair tied back in a ponytail, Elena's fitted police uniform was topped with a sleek black vest, also equipped with additional pouches for ammunition and tactical gear like a first aid kit. She carried her Sig Sauer in a thigh holster and had a radio clipped to her shoulder for easy communication.

Tom also wore a tactical vest, complete with gear such as flashbang grenades and extra ammunition. He had chosen a Smith & Wesson M&P Shield as his sidearm. Similarly equipped, Baxter carried a Beretta 92FS holstered at his hip and had a radio clipped to his vest.

The SWAT team stood ready in their full tactical gear. Clad in black with armored vests and helmets, they projected an intimidating image. Their vests were loaded with an array of essential gear and each member carried a Heckler & Koch MP5 submachine gun.

Rafael stood in the center of the group, his hands cuffed in front of him and an eye mask fastened over his eyes. Deprived of his sight, his arrogance seemed diminished. The blindfold was a necessary precaution to prevent him from identifying their route or the location of the safe house.

Captain Rodriguez approached, her hair pulled back into a tight bun.

"Listen up," she said. "This is a top-priority mission and Rafael is a crucial asset. We need to move fast and stay vigilant."

She motioned for Lucas to step aside, wanting a private word. Lucas followed her to a quieter corner of the garage, his curiosity piqued by her urgency. "Captain?"

Rodriguez reached into her jacket and pulled out a satellite phone, pressing it into his palm.

"Lucas, this is your lifeline. You use this once—only if you hit an emergency you can't handle."

"Understood," Lucas said, his fingers closing around the device.

"Keep this close," Rodriguez advised, her tone dropping lower. "We still don't know who the mole is, and that makes this operation vulnerable. The mole could be anyone."

"Anyone in particular?"

"It could even be someone on your team." Rodriguez's eyes flickered with concern. "Watch your back and keep an eye on Elena."

"Elena?" Lucas frowned.

"Her brother, Miguel. There's chatter he might be tangled up with The Phantom's ring." Rodriguez's words were like a punch to the gut. "It doesn't mean she's involved, but family ties... they can complicate things."

"I see," Lucas muttered.

"Lucas, she's your partner. But don't let your guard down," Rodriguez insisted.

"Understood," Lucas replied, pocketing the satellite phone.

"Good. Remember, we need Rafael if we're going to take down Gabriel Sandoval. Keep him secure and keep him anonymous. I'll be monitoring from here and coordinating any backup you need. Keep your regular communication lines open."

Lucas nodded again. "We'll check in regularly."

Rodriguez glanced back at the group, her eyes lingering on Rafael. "Don't let Rafael slip away."

"We won't," Lucas assured her.

Rodriguez gave him a final nod before stepping back. "Good luck. I'll be here if you need anything."

Lucas returned to the group. He exchanged a quick look with Elena, who raised an eyebrow questioningly.

"Everything alright?" Elena asked.

"Just a final pep talk," Lucas replied, a faint smile touching his lips. "Let's get this done. The SWAT armored van will lead; Elena, Rafael, and I will be in the second car; Tom and Baxter in the third."

The team moved into action. The SWAT officers formed a protective cordon around Rafael as they escorted him to Lucas' car. Tom and Baxter assumed their positions in the third vehicle.

Lucas watched as Elena slid into the driver's seat. He opened the rear door for Rafael, who looked disoriented by the blindfold. "In you go," Lucas directed.

"Feels like I'm diving into the abyss," Rafael mumbled, as he settled into the backseat.

"Shut up," Lucas said, climbing in beside him. He clipped Rafael's seatbelt into place.

"Check, check," Baxter's voice crackled through the radio. "Car Three to Car Two, all systems are go."

"Copy that, Baxter. Keep your eyes peeled," Elena replied. Lucas heard the engine of the third car purr to life behind them. Elena's fingers curled around the ignition key, and the engine of the Ford Explorer purred to life. She checked the rearview mirror, her gaze meeting Lucas's reflection—a nod passed between them.

"Are we ready?" Elena asked.

"Let's roll out," Lucas confirmed, checking his sidearm discreetly. He felt the weight of the satellite phone against his thigh—a lifeline he hoped he wouldn't need to use.

Elena eased the vehicle into the procession behind the armored SWAT van. The convoy pulled out of the garage and into the dark streets. The city was quiet at this hour, the streets empty and the buildings looming like silent sentinels.

Lucas turned to Rafael, whose chest rose and fell with a rhythm that hinted at the anxiety churning beneath his calm exterior.

"Easy, Rafael," Lucas murmured. "Just sit tight and be quiet."

He went over the route again in his mind, tracing invisible lines on an unseen map, pinpointing where trouble might brew.

"Streets are clear," Elena broke the silence.

"Let's keep it that way," Lucas replied.

The high-rises bled into squat buildings as they edged closer to the city limits. Lucas spotted the neon flicker of a dingy motel sign, one he'd surveilled during an undercover op years back.

"Almost there," Lucas muttered.

"Counting on it," Elena replied.

"Any tails?" Lucas peered over his shoulder, scanning the sparse traffic for the telltale signs of pursuit.

"Negative. We're ghosting them, just like we planned."

Chapter 22

The late evening sky was deep indigo, dotted with stars as the convoy sliced through the humid Miami air. The hum of the car engine was the only sound until Lucas's phone buzzed in his pocket. He glanced at the screen, frowning as he saw the caller ID: Gabriel Sandoval. Through the rearview mirror, he exchanged a concerned look with Elena before answering the call, putting it on speaker so she could hear.

"This is Detective Grant."

"Detective Grant, what a pleasure," Gabriel's smooth voice came through the speaker. "I hope you're having a pleasant evening."

"Cut to the chase, Gabriel. What do you want?"

Gabriel chuckled. "Straight to business, I see. Very well. I have a proposition for you. Release my son Rafael, and I'll make it worth your while. One million dollars each for you and your partner. Think about it—financial freedom for the rest of your lives."

"We're not interested in your bribes, Gabriel. Rafael will face justice, and so will you."

Gabriel's tone turned cold. "You're making a big mistake, Detective. Refusing my offer is unwise. Do you know what I can do to you, your family, and your partner?"

Through the rearview mirror, Elena's eyes met Lucas's, her expression resolute. She nodded, silently urging him to stand firm.

"We're not afraid of you, Gabriel," Lucas said. "Your threats mean nothing. If you want to avoid more bloodshed, you should surrender yourself to the police. It's the only way this ends without more violence."

There was a moment of silence on the other end, and Lucas could almost hear Gabriel's calculating mind working through the options.

"You're a brave man, Detective Grant," Gabriel said finally. "But bravery can quickly turn into foolishness. My reach is long, and my resources are vast. I can make your lives very difficult. You know, at that delightful event on my golf course, I could've taken you and your pretty partner out so easily."

Lucas took a deep breath, his mind racing. He knew Gabriel was serious, but he also knew they couldn't back down. "We're doing our jobs, Gabriel. Turn yourself in, cooperate with the investigation, and maybe you can negotiate a deal. Bribery and threats won't get you anywhere."

Gabriel's laugh was dark and humorless. "You think you can win this, don't you? You're more naïve than I thought.

But I respect your determination. Just remember, Detective, everyone has a breaking point. You and your partner—be careful."

The call ended abruptly, the silence in the car now deafening.

"What do you think?" Elena asked.

"Something's off," Lucas said, his detective instincts flaring into overdrive. "Alert the team, high alert."

Elena nodded, reaching for the radio. "All units, eyes wide. Something may be coming."

As she relayed the message, Lucas fumbled for his phone, punching in the number for Captain Rodriguez. It rang once, twice, then fell into the abyss of her voicemail.

"Captain, it's Lucas," he said tersely after the tone. "Gabriel Sandoval just called me. He wants his son released and threatens the team. Call me back ASAP."

"Stay sharp, Elena," Lucas muttered, his eyes darting between the road ahead and the mirrors. "He's planning something, and we're right in the thick of it."

The tranquility of the night was shattered by a deafening explosion. An RPG streaked out of the darkness, striking the SWAT armored van at the front of the convoy. A fiery blast ripped through the vehicle's reinforced exterior. The van lifted off the ground, its heavy frame twisting violently in the air. It tumbled end over end, a grotesque ballet of metal and flame, before crashing down on its roof with a thunderous impact, sliding several yards before coming to a smoking halt.

Elena's heart pounded in her chest as she swerved to avoid the wreckage. "Ambush!" she shouted.

Ahead of them, two vehicles screeched to a halt, blocking the road. Lucas glanced in the rearview mirror and saw another pair of vehicles closing in from behind, boxing them in.

"Shit!" Rafael shouted from the back seat, his voice a mix of shock and fear.

"Down!" Lucas barked, pressing himself into the seat.

"It's a trap," Lucas said tersely, drawing his weapon.

Rafael's voice rose in panic, "You can't just shoot your way out of this! Just give me up and I promise they won't hurt you."

"Shut up!" Elena snapped back.

"Elena, keep driving! Push through!" Lucas said.

"Tom, Baxter, lay down cover fire!" Lucas barked into the mic, his words punctuated by the sharp report of his weapon firing through the window.

Through the rear window, he saw Tom and Baxter spring into action. Their car doors flung open as they rolled out. Tom crouched behind the wrecked hulk of the armored van, his rifle spitting bullets into the darkness. Baxter found his perch on the other side, firing rapidly at the attackers. The staccato rhythm of their weapons formed a deadly chorus with Lucas's.

"Elena, left, now!" Lucas barked.

Elena wrenched the wheel sharply to the left, tires screeching in protest against the asphalt as they barreled down a dark side road.

"Are we clear?" Elena shouted over her shoulder, scanning the rearview mirror for any sign of pursuit.

Lucas peered through the rear window. "Can't tell—too much dust!"

"Damn it, we can't lead them to the safe house!" Lucas fumbled with his phone to relay new orders but found no signal. "Comms are jammed!"

"Any Plan B?" Elena took another sharp turn, the car's engine growling like an enraged beast.

"Continue heading south. Once we're far enough, we'll ditch the car."

Chapter 23

Lucas glanced back through the rear window. The road stretched out behind them, empty and dark except for the occasional beam of moonlight peering through the clouds above. He turned to Elena. "Pull over here. Turn off all lights and the engine."

Elena gave him a questioning look but complied, steering the Ford Explorer onto the gravel shoulder of the deserted road. As the vehicle shuddered to a stop, the only sound was the distant call of night creatures hidden within the dark landscape.

"Elena, I need to talk to you," Lucas said, popping the door open. The crisp air filled his lungs as he rounded the car to join Elena, her posture rigid with anticipation.

"Is everything okay?" she asked, peering into his face as they stood side by side, away from the earshot of the man handcuffed in the back seat.

Lucas took a deep breath, feeling the weight of his next words. "I need to ask you about Miguel."

"About Miguel?" Elena's brow furrowed, her arms crossing defensively. "What about him?"

"His involvement with The Phantom drug ring. What do you know about it?"

"Where did you hear that?"

"From Captain Rodriguez."

"Lucas, I—" Elena swallowed hard. "Miguel... he got in too deep. Started selling on campus to clear his debts."

Lucas watched her closely, noting the tremble in her voice and how her hands clutched at her sides.

"Debts to Gabriel Sandoval's crew?"

"Yes. I've spoken to him, Lucas. He's scared, but he wants out. He's willing to cooperate, to help us take Gabriel Sandoval down."

"Are you sure?"

"Absolutely. Miguel's made mistakes, but he's not beyond redemption."

"Why didn't you come to me?" Lucas asked.

"I was planning on bringing Miguel with me to discuss with you about his options, but then we had a breakthrough with capturing Vincent and became consumed with the case. Miguel's matter got pushed aside. I'm sorry," Elena explained.

Lucas nodded slowly, processing her words. He paced a few steps away from the car, the gravel crunching under his boots.

He stopped and turned to face her. "Elena, there's something else we need to clear up before we go any further."

"What is it?"

"Are you the mole?" His question sliced through the stillness between them.

Her silhouette stiffened. "What? Lucas, no!"

"Because if you are—" he started, but she cut him off.

Elena's hand recoiled as if scalded, her dark eyes swimming with betrayal. "Lucas, everything we've been through together—how could you?" Her voice trembled. "You know me. You know my dedication to this badge, to justice. We've been in the trenches together, faced down barrels of guns, and you think I could... betray all of that?"

He exhaled slowly. "I had to ask, Elena. We've been blindsided too many times lately." He stepped closer, the gap between them shrinking until he could see the hurt flickering in her eyes—a hurt he'd inflicted.

"Elena, I'm sorry. The closer we get to Gabriel Sandoval, the more tangled this web becomes," he said softly, reaching out to bridge the distance between them. His fingers grazed her hand, a tentative touch seeking forgiveness. "Look at me. I believe you."

"Is that supposed to make me feel better?" She wrapped her arms around herself, a shield against the chill and the doubt he'd sown. "Our lives are on the line every day, Lucas. If we can't trust each other, what do we have left?"

Lucas took a step toward her. "I need to know where everyone stands, especially when it's someone as close to me as you are."

"Then you should know by now," Elena shot back. "My stand is here, with you, against them. Always has been."

Lucas nodded. He scanned the inky horizon, where the city's pulse throbbed at a distance, its lights mere glimmers against the velvet night. He turned back to Elena.

"Okay, listen. We need to lay low and vanish into thin air. Rafael is a walking target, and if Gabriel Sandoval's crew get to him, we lose our edge."

"Vanish? Lucas, that's easier said than done. We're not ghosts."

"Close enough," Lucas replied with a half-smirk. "I know a place, off the grid, with no connections to the department or our usual haunts. No one knows about it except me... and now you."

"What kind of place is it? How secure is this location?"

"It's very safe. You will like it when we arrive. Trust me, it's Fort Knox meets Alcatraz."

"Sounds cozy."

"Cozy's not my style. Safety is. And right now, it's what we need."

"So when do we move?"

"Now. The longer we wait, the more time they have to sniff us out. We need to change our clothes and go undercover."

"I have extra clothing in my bag," Elena said.

"Great. You take a break, and I will drive."

Together, they turned back toward the car.

Chapter 24

The early morning light was just beginning to break over the horizon as Lucas and Elena pulled their Ford Explorer into the small harbor facing the swamp. The dawn illuminated the mist that clung to the surface of the water like a delicate veil.

The main structure of the harbor was a long, weathered wooden dock that extended into the calm water. The wood was aged, but it held firm. The dock was lined with mooring posts, each one equipped with heavy-duty ropes and cleats to secure the various boats that bobbed gently in the water.

A small bait and tackle shop stood at the entrance, its wooden walls painted a faded blue and adorned with nautical decorations. Nets, buoys, and old fishing rods hung from the eaves, giving the shop a quaint feel. A sign above the door read "Swamp's Edge Bait & Tackle" in white letters.

Lucas's hand was a blur as it shot beneath the driver's seat, fingers tracing the familiar contours of the metal box hidden there. With a swift yank, the box gave way, clanging softly against the car floor. He flipped the latch, the lid springing open to reveal neat stacks of bills.

"Got it," Lucas muttered, slamming the lid shut and stuffing the cash into the duffle bag at his feet.

Elena hunched low in the passenger seat, cast a quick glance over her shoulder. "What are you doing?"

Lucas tossed the bag over his shoulder. "You stay in the car with Rafael. I am going to get us a boat."

"OK," she said.

They had ditched their phones miles back, anything that could be tracked or traced. Gabriel Sandoval knew how to hunt. Lucas wasn't about to leave a trail.

When Lucas stepped out of the car, he could hear the sounds of the harbor waking up. The distant call of birds echoed through the air, mingling with the gentle lapping of water against the dock. The air was fresh and cool, filled with the earthy scent of wetland vegetation.

He made his way toward the end of the dock. A small, weathered shack stood amidst a cluster of airboats. The airboats were an impressive sight, with their flat-bottomed hulls designed for navigating the shallow, reedy waters of the Everglades. Each boat was equipped with a large, elevated fan at the back, the powerful engine capable of propelling the boat over water and marshland alike. The fans were surrounded by protective cages, and the seats were high and sturdy, providing a clear view of the vegetation.

The sign above the door, painted in bold, faded letters, read "Airboats for Sale." An old man emerged from the shack as Lucas approached. His skin was tanned and leathery from years spent under the sun, and his eyes were sharp and assessing.

"Morning," the old man greeted him. "What can I do for you?"

"I need to buy an airboat, and I need it now."

The man raised an eyebrow. "You in some kind of hurry?"

"You could say that."

The man studied him for a moment longer before nodding. "Alright. Follow me."

He led Lucas to a nearby airboat, its aluminum hull glinting in the morning light. The boat was well-maintained, with a powerful engine and sturdy construction that promised reliability. Lucas inspected it, noting the details.

"This one's in good shape," the old man said, patting the side of the boat. "Got a full tank of gas and she's ready to go. Price is ten thousand."

Lucas didn't hesitate, pulling out a stack of cash from the duffle bag. "I'll take it."

The old man's eyes widened slightly at the sight of the money. He nodded, snatched the payment, and thumbed through the bills. "You know how to handle one of these?"

"Better than you think."

The old man handed over the keys. "Be careful out there. The swamp's a beautiful place, but it's also dangerous. Stick to the main channels, and keep an eye out for gators."

Lucas thanked him and tucked the key into his pocket. He turned on his heel and made his way back to the car. He opened the car door and removed Rafael's blindfold before pulling him out of the vehicle with his hands still bound behind his back. Rafael shot him a fierce look but kept quiet. Lucas then led Elena and Rafael to the waiting airboat.

After they secured Rafael on the airboat, Lucas turned to Elena. "We need to ditch the car. Can't risk anyone tracking us."

Elena nodded, her eyes scanning the harbor for any sign of trouble. "I'll take care of it."

Lucas watched as Elena drove the Ford Explorer down a deserted alley and disappeared. Moments later, she returned, jogging back to the dock.

"All set," she said.

Lucas nodded, turning his attention to the airboat.

"Where are we headed, Lucas?"

"My brother's place. He lives out in the swamp."

"Your brother? Will he help us?"

"James is an ex-marine who lives off the grid. It's the last place Gabriel will think to look for us. James will shelter us."

"Alright, then let's go."

Lucas settled into the pilot's seat of the airboat, his hand finding the ignition. The powerful fan roared to life, sending a spray of water into the air.

"Here we go." Lucas eased the boat away from the dock, the flat bottom skimming over the water. He pushed the throttle forward, and the airboat lurched, gliding away from the harbor into the vast expanse of the swamp.

"James better be ready for some company," Elena shouted over the din of the engine. "I never pictured my hideout to be in a swamp."

"Just wait till you meet the gators," Lucas managed a half-grin.

"Great. As long as they're not working for Gabriel."

The airboat sliced through the water. The wind lashed at them, ripping through Lucas's hair and pressing against Elena's face, forcing her eyes to narrow.

"Keep your head down!" Lucas yelled back to Elena.

"Got it!" Elena glanced over her shoulder to Rafael, who sat handcuffed on the airboat floor. His slicked-back hair was now a disheveled mess.

The swamp enveloped them completely now, thick vines and Spanish moss draping from twisted branches like nature's own barrier against the world they'd left behind. The air was thick with humidity, the sounds of wildlife creating a constant symphony around them as the airboat glided over the water. Lucas leaned into the helm, his eyes scanning for the hidden channels he knew existed within the labyrinthine waterways.

Rafael shifted uncomfortably, the handcuffs digging into his wrists. He glanced up at Elena, a desperate gleam in his eyes. "Detective Torres, this is all a big misunderstanding. I can make it worth your while if you let me go."

Elena didn't even blink. "Save your breath, Rafael. We're not interested."

Rafael leaned forward, his voice dropping to a conspiratorial whisper. "Come on, think about it. Name your price. I'll pay you whatever you want. A hundred grand? Two hundred? Just say the word."

Lucas glanced over his shoulder, his green eyes narrowing. "You're wasting your time, Rafael. We're not for sale."

Rafael shifted again, trying to find a more comfortable position on the hard floor. "Okay, fine. How about this? You let me go, and I'll give you each a million dollars. Tax-free. No questions asked. You can disappear, and live a life of luxury. Just think about it."

Elena crossed her arms, her expression hardening. "We're not letting you go. Not for a million, not for any amount of money. You're going to face justice."

Rafael's voice grew more frantic. "I can get you a mansion in the Keys. A yacht. Hell, I'll throw in a private jet. You could live like royalty. Just let me go. Please. Nobody will know."

Lucas cut the engine, the airboat drifting to a slow stop. He turned to face Rafael. "You think we're doing this for money? You think we're corruptible? You have no idea who you're dealing with."

Rafael swallowed hard. "Look, man, I'm just trying to make a deal here. I'm in a tight spot, okay?"

Elena stepped closer, her voice ice-cold. "We're not here to make deals, Rafael. We're here to make sure you pay for the lives you've destroyed with your drugs. Offering us bribes just proves how guilty you are."

Rafael's eyes darted between Lucas and Elena, his voice turning pleading. "Please, you don't understand. If I go down, my wife and daughter... they'll be in danger. You have to help me."

Lucas shook his head slowly. "You should have thought about that before you got involved in the drug business. We're not letting you walk away from this."

Rafael slumped back, the fight draining out of him. "You're making a mistake. You don't know what you're dealing with."

"Maybe we don't know everything. But we know enough to see this through. You're not getting away, Rafael," Elena said.

Lucas restarted the engine, the roar breaking the tense silence. The airboat resumed its journey, cutting through the swamp with purpose.

"Watch for gators," Lucas half-joked. "Wouldn't want one of them mistaking Rafael for breakfast."

Elena chuckled. "Considering how greasy he is, I doubt even the gators would want a bite of him."

Rafael glared at Elena but kept his mouth shut.

Chapter 25

The late afternoon sun cast a golden glow over the swamp as Lucas and Elena's airboat glided through the winding waterways. The dense foliage and towering cypress trees created a canopy overhead, their gnarled roots twisting into the murky water below. Lucas's grip on the rudder eased slightly. "We are almost there."

Elena leaned forward, her keen eyes scanning the shadowy outline of cypress trees and hanging moss that danced gently in the humid breeze. "Sounds good."

As they navigated the final bend, a large piece of land emerged, rising above the swamp. Atop this natural elevation stood a rugged house.

The house was a one-story structure built with a blend of rustic charm and practicality. The exterior was clad in weathered wood. A wide porch wrapped around the front and sides of the house, providing a place to sit and watch the ever-changing scenery of the swamp. The roof, made of corrugated metal, glinted softly in the fading light.

The house was elevated on thick wooden stilts, a precaution against the swamp's occasional flooding. Large windows adorned the walls, allowing natural light to flood the interior and offering panoramic views of the lush landscape.

The dock extended from the elevated land down to the water, built from sturdy planks of cypress wood. It was wide enough to accommodate multiple boats and lined with railings for safety. Lanterns hung from posts along the dock, ready to be lit as dusk approached.

Moored at the dock was another airboat, significantly larger than Lucas? Designed for transporting both people and cargo, its metal hull was polished and well-maintained. Cushioned seats and a sturdy canopy hinted at comfort during long trips, while the large fan and powerful engine at the rear promised speed and agility.

"James," Lucas called out.

As Lucas steered the airboat to the dock, a man appeared on the porch, his tall, broad-shouldered figure immediately recognizable. His piercing green eyes, similar to Lucas's, scanned the water with vigilance. He wore a plain T-shirt, and his rugged demeanor softened with a welcoming smile.

"Lucas," James called out, stepping down to the dock. "I figured you'd show up sooner or later."

Lucas killed the engine and hopped out, helping Elena and then Rafael onto the dock. Lucas pulled his brother into a firm hug. "It's good to see you."

James nodded, his eyes flicking to Elena and then to Rafael with a questioning look. "What's going on?"

"James, this is my partner, Detective Elena Torres," Lucas said, gesturing to Elena.

Elena stepped forward, extending a hand. "Nice to meet you, James."

James shook her hand. "Any friend of Lucas is welcome here."

Lucas looked around, taking in the familiar surroundings. "We need to lay low for a few days and keep Rafael out of sight until we can move him safely. Think we can stay here?"

James glanced at Rafael, who was trying to look as inconspicuous as possible. "No problem. You can stay as long as you need. The swamp's a good place to hide if you know your way around."

Rafael looked around the swamp. "This place gives me the creeps," he muttered.

James shot him a sharp look. "Better the creeps than a bullet in the head, don't you think?"

Rafael fell silent, realizing the truth in James's words.

"Detective Torres," James turned his attention to Elena. "I trust my little brother hasn't been too much of a pain?"

"Only on the best days," Elena responded with a half-smile. "You can just call me Elena."

"Come on inside, let's get you two into some dry clothes. You look like hell warmed over," James joked.

They made their way up the wooden steps and onto the porch. Inside, the house was filled with worn but comfortable furniture. The living room was dominated by a large sofa and a sturdy wooden table. Shelves lined the walls, filled with tools and various trinkets collected over the years. A deer head hung on the wall, adding a rustic charm to the overall decor. The air was cooler, a welcome respite from the swamp's heat and humidity.

"Make yourselves at home," James said.

"Do you have a secure room where we can detain Rafael?" Lucas asked.

James nodded. "Yeah, I've got a room that should work. Follow me."

James led them down a narrow hallway to a small room at the back of the house. The room was simple, consisting of a metal-framed twin bed and a solitary window.

Elena glanced at the window. "Can this window be an escape route?"

"I've got a security alarm system. If Rafael tries to get out through the window, we'll know. Besides, we're in the middle of the swamp. He has nowhere to go," James said.

Elena nodded, satisfied with the explanation.

"Can the room be locked?" Lucas asked.

James left the room briefly and returned with a key. "Here you go," he said, handing the key to Lucas. "This should keep him secure."

They guided Rafael into the room and sat him on the bed. The handcuffs clicked open, and Lucas gave him a stern look. "Don't even think about trying to escape, Rafael. The swamp will swallow you up before the gators can get to you. So just stay put. This room is your world until we say otherwise."

"May I have some water, Detective?"

Elena left the room and returned with a bottle of water for Rafael.

They stepped out of the room, closing the door behind them. Lucas turned the key in the lock, ensuring it was secure.

James watched them. "You sure you're okay with this?"

Lucas nodded, a grim smile on his face. "I think this is fine."

As they made their way back to the living room, Lucas could sense the tension slowly dissipating from his body. He sank into the plush sofa and took a deep breath. Elena sat down next to him, and he could feel the tension eased from her shoulders.

With a bottle of whiskey and two glasses in hand, James walked over to them. He poured the amber liquid, offering a small relief to their frayed nerves.

"Thanks, brother." Lucas accepted his glass.

"Cheers," Elena echoed.

"Here's to finding sanctuary." Lucas tipped his glass in James's direction.

"And keeping it," Elena added, as she took a long drink.

"Sanctuary it is," James agreed, settling into an armchair across from them.

The room fell silent save for the distant hum of life beyond the walls. James stepped outside to tend to the grill.

"When was the last time you were here?" Elena asked Lucas.

"A couple of years ago, on Thanksgiving," Lucas said, taking another sip of whiskey.

"I wonder how Tom, Baxter, and the SWAT team are doing," Elena said.

Lucas let out a heavy sigh. "We won't know until we get back. But they're all seasoned officers; I have faith in their abilities."

"Attacking the SWAT team? Gabriel's got balls," Elena said.

"He has declared war on law enforcement. He is digging his own grave," Lucas stated with conviction.

A few minutes later, James returned with a platter of grilled alligator meat, the aroma making Elena's mouth water. "Dinner's ready," he announced, placing the platter on the table. "Hope you like alligator meat. It's a local delicacy."

Elena's eyes widened with curiosity. "I've never had alligator meat before. It smells amazing."

They sat down to eat, the flavors of the tender, smoky meat delighting Elena's taste buds. "This is delicious." She smiled at James. "Thank you for the meal."

James chuckled. "Glad you like it. There's plenty more where that came from." He seated himself across from them at the wooden table. "Not quite a feast, but it'll do."

"How is Ava?" James asked Lucas.

"She's doing well."

"Do you think she misses her uncle?"

"I don't think so," Lucas said with a wink.

"I miss her, that little sweetheart."

"You should come visit us in Miami sometime. We could have some fun together," Lucas suggested.

"That sounds like a great idea."

Later, Lucas entered the small room where Rafael was confined and handed him a plate of food. Rafael took it in silence.

Chapter 26

After dinner, when the plates were cleared and the last remnants of daylight faded from the sky, James turned to Lucas. "You can take the sofa in the living room. It's not the most comfortable, but it'll do for the night."

"Thanks, James," Lucas said, his exhaustion apparent now that he allowed it to surface.

James led Elena to a small room. The space was modest, with a makeshift bed covered by a patchwork quilt and a small wooden dresser pressed against one wall. A window provided a view of the swamp outside.

"This will be your room," James said, gesturing to the bed. "It's not much, but it's quiet and comfortable."

Elena smiled. "It's perfect. Thank you, James."

"Bathrooms at the end of the hall. Get some rest. You'll need your energy for whatever comes next."

After James left, Elena lay back on the bed, the makeshift mattress surprisingly comfortable. The gentle symphony of the swamp lulled her into a peaceful sleep, the worries of the day fading away.

In the living room, Lucas settled onto the sofa, pulling a blanket over himself. His thoughts drifted to the case, to Rafael locked up just rooms away. But the weariness won out, pulling him under. Within minutes, Lucas succumbed to sleep, his breath steady and deep.

The night was thick, and the humid air was heavy with the scent of damp earth. The occasional rustle of leaves and the distant croak of a frog were the only sounds breaking the silence.

Inside the house, the sudden blare of the security alarm jolted everyone awake. James rushed to the security panel near the front door. His eyes widened as he read the display.

"Rafael's room," James shouted.

Lucas and Elena followed James down the hallway to Rafael's room. The door flew open, revealing an empty room. The twin bed was undisturbed, but the small window was wide open, the screen torn away.

"Damn it," Lucas muttered. He grabbed his Glock, handcuffs, and a flashlight from his bag. Without hesitation, he jumped out of the window, landing with a soft thud on the damp ground outside.

Elena and James ran out of the front door, their flashlights slicing through the inky darkness. The beams of light danced across the swamp, revealing dense foliage, twisted tree roots, and the occasional glint of water.

The air was thick with humidity, each breath heavy with the scent of moss and stagnant water. Lucas moved swiftly, his flashlight beam scanned the area around the house. The swamp was a labyrinth of shadows, each one a potential hiding place for Rafael.

"Rafael!" Lucas called out. "There's nowhere to run! Come back, and we can sort this out!"

There was no response, only the unsettling stillness of the swamp.

Elena and James circled the house, their beams of light crossing and re-crossing each other as they searched. "Rafael, you can't hide forever!" Elena shouted.

The swamp seemed to swallow their voices. The occasional splash of a frog jumping into the water or the rustle of a nocturnal creature moving through the underbrush were the only responses.

"He can't have gone far," James said. "This swamp is unforgiving. He won't last long out here."

Suddenly, Lucas's flashlight caught a glimmer of movement—a brief flash of something in the darkness. He moved toward it, his heart racing. "Elena! James! Over here!"

They converged on Lucas's position, their flashlights illuminating the area. But the glimmer of movement had disappeared, swallowed by the night once more. They stood there, frustrated.

Lucas's flashlight beam caught a sudden movement ahead, and he froze. Two large alligators lay partially submerged in a murky pool, their eyes reflecting the light in an eerie glow. The alligators were massive, easily twelve feet long, their thick, leathery bodies covered in rough, dark scales that glistened with moisture. Their powerful tails lay motionless behind them, and their broad, muscular legs ended in sharp, deadly claws.

The alligators' heads were lifted slightly above the water, their long, pointed snouts revealing rows of sharp teeth. Their eyes, set high on their heads, were fixed on Lucas. The larger of the two had a deep scar running along its side.

Lucas's heart pounded in his chest as he took in the sight of the enormous reptiles. He knew how dangerous they could be, especially when cornered or threatened. He took a step back, raising his free hand to signal Elena and James to halt.

"Stay calm," James whispered. "We need to scare them off."

The alligators reacted to the beam of the flashlight with a low, rumbling hiss, their mouths opening to reveal more of their fearsome teeth. They held their ground, their eyes locked on Lucas, their bodies tensed as if ready to strike.

Lucas knew he had to act quickly. He grabbed a nearby branch. Using it as a club, he started banging it against a tree, creating a loud, rhythmic noise that echoed through the swamp. At the same time, he waved the flashlight back and forth, trying to create a sense of movement and disturbance.

"Go on, get out of here!" Lucas shouted.

The alligators hesitated for a moment, their eyes still fixed on Lucas. But the combination of the noise and the erratic light seemed to unnerve them. With another low hiss, the larger alligator turned and slowly slid back into the water, its massive tail creating ripples that spread out across the surface. The second alligator followed suit until both had disappeared beneath the murky depths.

Lucas let out a breath he hadn't realized he was holding, lowering the branch and turning to Elena and James. "Alright, they're gone. Let's keep moving."

Elena nodded. "We need to find Rafael before he gets too far. He won't survive out here for long."

James tightened his grip on his flashlight. "It's dangerous out here at night. We have to hurry."

"Where could he have gone?" Elena asked.

Suddenly, a thought struck Lucas like a bolt of lightning. "The airboats! It's the only way for him to escape. We need to check the dock."

Without another word, they sprinted through the dense underbrush, their flashlights bobbing wildly as they navigated the uneven terrain.

They arrived at the dock, where the airboats were gently swaying on the water. Lucas's heart raced as he surveyed the surroundings. "Elena, James, get on my airboat and check everywhere," he said. "I'll take James's airboat."

Elena and James nodded, quickly boarding Lucas's airboat. They searched every nook and cranny, their flashlights slicing through the darkness, but there was no sign of Rafael.

Meanwhile, Lucas jumped onto James's airboat, his eyes scanning the shadows. He moved carefully, his flashlight revealing only empty spaces. Suddenly, a noise caught his attention—a slight rustle, a breath too loud to be the wind.

Before Lucas could react, Rafael sprang from a hiding place beneath some tarps. The force of his leap knocked Lucas off balance, and they both tumbled to the floor of the airboat, grappling in the darkness. The boat rocked precariously as they wrestled, their grunts and the sounds of their struggle the only things breaking the silence of the night.

Rafael fought desperately, his eyes wild with fear and determination. Lucas tightened his grip, using his strength and training to subdue Rafael. With a powerful punch, Lucas struck Rafael in the face, the impact breaking his nose. Rafael cried out in pain, blood streaming from his nose as he stopped resisting.

"Enough!" Lucas shouted. "It's over, Rafael."

Rafael nodded, gasping for air. "Okay, okay."

Lucas turned Rafael around, securing his wrists with handcuffs. He stood, pulling Rafael to his feet.

Elena and James stood anxiously at the edge of the dock. Relief washed over their faces as they saw Rafael in cuffs.

"Let's get him back to the house," Lucas said.

Together, they ushered Rafael back to the house. They laid Rafael on the twin bed, his face still smeared with blood from his broken nose, his eyes reflecting a blend of pain and defeat.

Lucas looked at him, his expression hard. "Try anything like that again, and it won't end well for you."

He took the handcuffs and secured Rafael's wrist to the metal bed frame, ensuring they were tight enough to prevent any further escape attempts. "Without the keys, the airboats won't start, OK? Why don't you do yourself a favor and just stay put? Otherwise, you will get yourself killed."

"I get it." Rafael winced.

Lucas straightened and turned to James. "We need to make sure he can't use that window again. Do you have anything to board it up?"

"I'll get some wood planks and tools. We'll make sure he stays put this time," James said and left the room.

Moments later, James returned carrying several wooden planks, two hammers, and a box of nails. "Let's get this done," he said, handing Lucas a hammer and some nails.

They worked quickly, boarding up the small window with the planks. Elena stood by the door, keeping an eye on Rafael.

Once the window was boarded up, Lucas and James stepped back, inspecting their work. The planks were solid, leaving no gaps that Rafael could exploit. The room felt even smaller now.

"You're not going anywhere," Lucas said to Rafael.

Rafael nodded silently, his eyes downcast. They stepped out of the room, Lucas turning the key in the lock, ensuring it was secure.

Chapter 27

The first light of dawn kissed the horizon, casting a soft glow over the swamp as Lucas' eyes snapped open. The chirping of crickets was giving way to the morning calls of birds, a natural alarm clock that stirred him from sleep. He rolled out of the sofa, his thoughts already set on the upcoming day.

"Rise and shine," Lucas muttered, nudging the slumbering form of Elena, who lay in the makeshift bed in her room.

"Five more minutes," she mumbled, the words muffled by her pillow.

Lucas chuckled. "Swamp waits for no one, Detective."

With a groan, Elena sat up, raking her fingers through her dark hair. "I'm up, I'm up," she conceded, throwing off the blanket.

James was already outside and checked the contents of their cooler.

"Got enough bait?" Lucas asked, stepping into the cool air.

"Enough to catch a feast," James replied with a grin, handing Lucas a thermos of coffee. "You ready to leave narcotics behind for a day?"

"More than ready." Lucas took a deep sip.

"Let's make sure we have everything," Elena said as she joined them, lacing up her boots with nimble fingers. "Rods, reels, tackle box, mosquito spray... what about sunscreen? You know how you burn, Lucas."

Lucas patted his pocket, producing a tube with a flourish. "Wouldn't dream of forgetting it," he said, earning an approving nod from Elena.

"Let's get everything loaded up," James said.

They stowed the rods and reels on James' airboat along with the tackle box and cooler.

"Looks like we're all set," Elena announced.

"Today, it's just us and the fish," Lucas said, a half-smile playing on his lips. "No cases, no perps, just the swamp."

"Good. Because I plan on catching the biggest bass and showing you boys how it's done," Elena said.

"Alright, let's shove off," James declared.

Lucas's hands tightened on the controls of the airboat as he turned the key in the ignition. The engine roared to life, and the boat glided through the water as the sun's early rays stretched out long shadows around them.

The swamp was a sprawling network of narrow channels. The soft buzz of insects, the distant call of a heron, and the occasional splash of a fish breaking the surface created a soothing backdrop. Dragonflies darted above the water, their iridescent wings catching the light as they moved in erratic patterns.

"Take this left up ahead," James said, pointing toward a break in the dense foliage. "There's a spot about half a mile through there. Always had good luck."

"Got it." Lucas angled the airboat into the channel.

They glided past a thick stand of cattails, their slender stalks swaying gently in the breeze. The water here was clear and shallow, revealing clusters of lily pads floating on the surface, their broad, flat leaves interspersed with delicate white and pink flowers.

They reached a secluded lagoon, its waters calm and still. The lagoon was bordered by a mix of cypress and mangrove trees, their roots intertwining to form natural barriers. Small fish darted in the shallows, while larger shadows beneath the surface hinted at the presence of their quarry.

James nodded. "This is the spot. Lots of cover for the bass, and plenty of food."

Lucas cut the engine, allowing the boat to drift to a gentle stop. He and James began setting up their fishing gear, while Elena took in the serene beauty of the surroundings.

"This place is so peaceful," Elena said softly.

James smiled, his hands deftly baiting a hook. "That's the beauty of the swamp. It's a hidden world, untouched by all the noise and rush. Just you, the swamp, and the fish."

Lucas peered over the side, catching sight of shadows flickering beneath the surface. "So, what's the secret?" he asked, reaching for his rod.

"Precision." James picked up his rod. "You want to get right on the edge—right there," he pointed with the tip of his rod to the space where greenery met open water, "where they're lurking for prey."

"Predators in hiding," Lucas mused, threading a lure onto his line.

"Exactly. And patience," James continued. "Just like tracking down leads. Wait for them to come to you."

"Something I'm good at," Lucas said, casting his line with a smooth, arching motion. The lure landed softly beside the lilies, sending ripples across the glassy surface.

"Nice throw," James acknowledged, casting his line out.

Lucas settled back and fixed his gaze where the tiny waves emanated from the lure.

"Watch the way the water moves," James said in a low voice. "Differentiate between the natural flow and the telltale signs of a nibble."

"Like distinguishing a false lead from the real deal," Lucas murmured, almost to himself.

Silence draped over them, broken only by the occasional creak of the boat or the plop of a frog leaping to safety.

Elena stepped up to the boat's edge, gripping her rod. She glanced over at Lucas, who was already in his element.

"Mind if I show you how it's done?" Elena teased.

"By all means, Detective," Lucas replied. "Enlighten me."

She surveyed the expanse of water before them, her eyes narrowing slightly as she calculated the trajectory. With a fluid motion, Elena flicked her wrist, sending the line sailing through the air. It landed with a soft plop, well beyond where Lucas' had settled. Elena gave Lucas a sidelong smile filled with friendly challenges.

"Precision," she said, "it's not just for the shooting range."

"Seems like you've got some hidden talents," Lucas acknowledged.

The surface of the swamp lay still, barely a ripple distorting its mirrored facade.

Lucas's muscles tensed, the line thrumming like a live wire in his hands. "Got something!" he exclaimed.

James stood up, leaning forward to get a better look. "That's it, brother! Reel that bad boy in!"

The Largemouth Bass surged, fighting for freedom, but Lucas matched its fervor with an unyielding grip and steady cranks of the reel.

"Easy..." Elena said, eyes tracking the rod's arc. "Don't snap the line."

"Trust me," Lucas grunted, his arms working rhythmically.

With a defiant leap, the fish broke the surface, droplets of water catching the sunlight like tiny prisms before it slapped against the side of the boat. Lucas leaned down, securing the bass with his hands, and lifted his conquest.

"Ha! Look at the size of this one!" he beamed, holding the bass up. Its scales threw back the light, creating a shimmering spectacle.

"Damn fine catch, Lucas!" James clapped him on the shoulder.

"Alright, alright, you've set the bar," Elena said. She cast her line again, the lure arcing gracefully through the air before kissing the water's surface, barely causing a ripple.

"Your turn, Torres. Show us what you've got," Lucas teased.

"Watch, Grant," she shot back playfully.

The sun climbed higher, dappling the water with light, turning the waiting game into a meditation.

"Got another!" Elena's voice cut through the stillness. The fishing line cut through the water, taut and fast, creating small waves in its wake.

"Keep the tension," Lucas advised.

With a grunt of effort, Elena hauled back, and a Largemouth Bass burst from the water, thrashing wildly at the end of the line. She reeled in the fish to the boat where James scooped it up in a net.

"Nice technique, Elena," James complimented, admiring the bass before adding it to their growing collection in the cooler.

"But I'm still one behind you two." She wiped her brow.

"Let's make it a fair game then," Lucas said, casting his line back into the water.

"Lucas, right there, by the cypress knees. They love hiding out there," James pointed out.

Lucas adjusted his position and aimed his cast toward the tangled roots where shadows danced.

In no time, Lucas felt a tug on his line, followed by another, before feeling the energy of a bass fighting against him.

"Feels like a strong one," he grunted as he leaned into the pull.

"Bring it home," Elena encouraged.

"Another for the Grant brothers," James said, chuckling as he stored the fish with the others. Their cooler was now brimming with the day's efforts.

"Think we've got enough for a feast?" Elena asked.

"Definitely," Lucas replied, "James, let's head back."

"Okay." James took control, steering the airboat back toward home.

"Good day, huh?" Elena leaned back, letting the rush of wind comb through her hair.

"The best," Lucas agreed. "Nothing beats this—friends, family, and nature."

"Let's get these beauties ready for dinner." James smiled.

Chapter 28

Inside the kitchen, Elena rolled up her sleeves and scaled the bass on the weathered wooden counter.

James leaned against the counter. "Need any help, Detective?"

"Actually, I could use some herbs. Do you have any?"

"Yeah, I've got a stash somewhere. Give me a minute."

"Watch and learn, Lucas," Elena quipped, a playful smirk dancing on her lips as she glanced over her shoulder at Lucas, who was leaning against the doorframe.

"Every time I think I've seen all your talents..." Lucas said, shaking his head in admiration.

"Don't get too excited yet. We'll see how it turns out."

James returned with a small tin filled with dried herbs. "Here you go. Hope these work."

Elena opened the tin, inhaling the fragrant mix of thyme, rosemary, and basil. "Perfect," she said, sprinkling the herbs over the fish.

"Where'd you learn to cook like that?" James asked.

"My grandmother taught me. She was an amazing cook, and she always said that good food brings people together."

"Elena, you could moonlight as a chef," Lucas marveled as the aroma began to build, growing richer with each passing moment.

"Stick with me, and you'll never need a restaurant again." Elena gave the fillets a deft flip, revealing a crispy golden crust.

"Good thing we caught enough to feed an army," James said, pulling plates from the cupboard. "I have a feeling we're going to want seconds."

"Or thirds," Lucas added.

As the fish sizzled in the pan, Lucas and James set the table. The wooden table was soon covered with plates, cutlery, and glasses filled with wine.

Elena plated the bass, garnishing it with a final sprinkle of herbs. "Dinner's ready," she announced, carrying the plates to the table.

"Here's to a job well done," Lucas toasted, lifting his glass.

James clinked his glass against Lucas's with a broad grin. "And to the best fishing trip this side of the Everglades."

"Only the best for you guys," Elena said, settling into her seat.

"Look at you two," James teased, his gaze flickering between Lucas and Elena. "Out there today, I swear, if I didn't know any better, I'd say you were an old married couple the way you bicker and banter."

Lucas's fork paused midway to his mouth, a smirk playing on his lips as he glanced at Elena.

"Ha, very funny," Elena shot back, though the blush on her cheeks betrayed her amusement.

"Never thought I'd say this, but swamp fishing might just be my new favorite pastime," Lucas said, spearing a flaky piece of fish with his fork.

Elena dabbed a napkin at the corner of her lips. "It's not about the catch, is it?"

Lucas nodded in agreement. "It's about the peace it brings. Out here, we're just three people enjoying the simple things—no case files, no leads to chase. Peace is fleeting in our line of work. We have to savor it while we can."

"Cheers to that," Elena said, lifting her glass.

***

The remnants of dinner lay scattered across the table. James excused himself to take a phone call, leaving Lucas and Elena alone in the kitchen. The warm glow from the overhead light cast a cozy ambiance over the room as they began to clean up.

Elena stood at the sink, rinsing dishes while Lucas dried them and put them away.

"I have fun today," Elena said, glancing at Lucas with a small smile.

Lucas returned the smile, his eyes lingering on her for a moment longer than usual. "Me too."

When Elena handed Lucas a plate, their fingers brushed. She felt a jolt of electricity run through her at the brief contact. Lucas looked up, his eyes meeting hers.

"Elena," Lucas said softly, his voice filled with an emotion she couldn't quite place.

Without thinking, Elena closed the small distance between them. Lucas's eyes darkened with intensity as he set the dish down and reached out, his hand gently cupping her cheek. The air between them crackled with anticipation.

"Lucas," she whispered, her voice barely audible over the pounding of her heart.

He leaned in, his lips brushing hers tentatively at first, then with increasing urgency. Elena responded, wrapping her arms around his neck as their kiss deepened. All the tension, the unspoken feelings, and the bond they had shared over the years came to the surface at that moment.

Lucas's hands moved to her waist, pulling her closer, while Elena's fingers tangled in his hair. The world outside the kitchen faded away, leaving just the two of them, lost in each other.

Lucas's hands traveled up Elena's back, stroking the small of her back before sliding under her shirt to caress her soft skin. She gasped into the kiss as his fingers found their way to her bare stomach then higher until they cupped her breasts. She moaned into his mouth at the touch, arching into his hand as he squeezed gently. Her nipples hardened beneath his fingers, and he couldn't help but roll them between his thumbs and forefingers. A shiver ran through him at the sensation.

When they finally broke apart, both were breathing heavily, their foreheads resting together. Lucas looked into Elena's eyes, a mix of wonder and desire in his gaze.

"I've wanted to do this for a long time," he admitted.

Elena smiled, her heart soaring. "Me too."

Lucas picked her up from the waistline and carried her to the makeshift bed. They were both naked within seconds.

Her eyes locked onto his as he leaned over her. His hands traced lines down her body, drawing patterns on her soft skin as if he were painting a masterpiece. He pushed her thighs apart, exposing her wet folds to his hungry gaze. Elena watched in anticipation as Lucas lowered himself between them, taking his member in one hand and guiding it toward her entrance.

Elena's heart raced as she felt the head of his cock tease at her entrance. With a swift thrust, he was inside of her—filling her with his hardness. A deep moan escaped her lips as she arched her back to accommodate him better. He was thick and heavy inside of her, stretching her walls in an exquisite pain that sent shockwaves of pleasure coursing through every nerve ending in her body.

His powerful hips pumped relentlessly, slamming into hers in a furious rhythm that made the whole bed shake beneath them. Lucas thrust into her with such intensity that Elena struggled to catch her breath. Her chest heaved up and down as her eyes shut tight and her lips parted, the occasional moan escaping them.

Lucas moved faster and faster, pounding into her. He could feel his testicles tightening, his member throbbing and spurting out hot semen into her depths. She held onto him tightly as her climax shook through her body.

He slumped on top of her, breathing heavily.

"I love you, Elena," Lucas whispered against her neck.

"I love you too, Lucas," she panted in response.

Chapter 29

Lucas's sleep was fractured by the urgent shake of a hand on his shoulder. His eyes snapped open to the dim outline of James.

"Lucas, wake up. We've got company."

Lucas was instantly alert, swinging his legs off the sofa and reaching for his clothes. "What's going on?"

James moved to the window, peering out cautiously. "Three large airboats just pulled up at the dock. They're heavily armed."

Lucas joined him at the window, his heart sinking as he saw the men disembarking from the airboats. Gabriel Sandoval stood at the forefront. He wore a tactical vest over a dark shirt, the vest bristling with weapons and ammunition. A sleek, semi-automatic rifle was slung over his shoulder, and a pistol was holstered at his hip. His face was set in a mask of cold determination, his piercing eyes scanning the area.

Behind Gabriel, his crew moved with the confidence of trained operatives. There were about a dozen of them, each one armed to the teeth. They wore black vests, cargo pants, and combat boots. Each man carried a combination of automatic rifles, shotguns, and sidearms, their movements coordinated as they spread out from the airboats.

One of the men, a hulking figure with a shaved head and a jagged scar running down his cheek, barked orders to the others. He carried a pump-action shotgun, the weapon's barrel glinting ominously in the pre-dawn light.

James woke Elena, explaining the situation in hushed tones. Elena's eyes narrowed as she processed the information.

"They have found us. They're here for Rafael," Lucas said, reaching for the satellite phone on the nightstand. He punched in a series of numbers and waited for Captain Rodriguez to pick up on the other end.

"Captain Rodriguez, it's Lucas. We're at my brother's swamp house and we've got incoming hostile."

"Lucas, are you okay?" Rodriguez's voice came through the line. "How many hostiles are there? Do you have a visual?"

"I count ten heavily armed men outside," Lucas said. "We need backup immediately."

"Backup's on its way, but it won't be immediate. You know how isolated you are out there. Hold the fort, Lucas. Leave the satellite phone on."

"Understood, Captain." Lucas ended the call. He turned to Elena and James. "Help's coming, but we're on our own until then."

"Let's get ready to give them a warm welcome then," Elena said.

"We're surrounded," Lucas said. "James, do you have any long guns?"

James nodded. "Follow me."

James led them to a hidden compartment on the floor, revealing a gun safe. He opened the safe and pulled out three assault rifles, along with several magazines of ammunition.

"Here," James said, handing a rifle to Lucas and another to Elena. "These should give us a fighting chance."

Lucas took the rifle, checking the magazine and the sights. Both he and Elena geared up with tactical vests. From a nearby closet, James retrieved a vest for himself and put it on.

Elena helped Lucas adjust his vest, her fingers brushing against his chest for a brief moment.

"Is it too tight?" Elena asked.

"No, it's perfect," Lucas replied, his hand gently covering hers.

The world outside ceased to exist as Lucas pulled Elena into a fierce embrace. Their lips crushed together in a frantic kiss, fueled by raw emotions and a need for comfort and strength from one another. At that moment, nothing else mattered except the all-consuming intensity of their love.

James cleared his throat loudly. "Hate to interrupt, lovebirds, but we've got a bit of a situation out here."

Lucas and Elena broke apart, their faces flushed. "Right," Lucas said. "Let's get ready. They've got us outnumbered and outgunned, but we have the home-court advantage."

Elena nodded. "We should stay inside. We can use Rafael as a shield. Gabriel won't risk shooting at his son."

James looked at her, a flicker of doubt in his eyes. "Are you sure about that? Gabriel's a ruthless bastard. He might not care."

"Rafael is the key to his empire. He won't risk losing him," Elena said.

Lucas' mind raced as he formulated a plan. "We'll use Rafael as leverage. But we need to be ready to fight if it comes to that. Our strategy is to delay them and hold out until reinforcements arrive."

Lucas moved swiftly through the dimly lit house and entered Rafael's room. Rafael lay on the bed, handcuffed to the metal frame, his eyes widened with confusion.

"We need to move," Lucas said. "Stay quiet, and do exactly as I say."

He unlocked the handcuffs from the bed frame and pulled Rafael to his feet. He re-secured the cuffs around Rafael's wrists, ensuring they were tight.

"Let's go," Lucas said, guiding Rafael out of the room and into the living room where Elena and James were making final preparations for the inevitable confrontation.

"Elena, stay close and make sure he doesn't try anything," Lucas said. "We need him alive."

"I've got him," Elena said, her weapon ready.

The fear in Rafael's eyes was palpable, but there was also a glimmer of hope.

James peered through a window. "They're getting closer. We don't have much time."

Elena positioned Rafael on the floor behind the couch, using the furniture as a makeshift cover. "Stay down and don't move," Elena ordered. Rafael nodded, his face pale.

The house was small, but they had fortified it as best they could, using furniture to create barriers and blocking off potential entry points.

Gabriel Sandoval's voice echoed through the trees, amplified by a bullhorn. "Detective Grant! Detective Torres! You're surrounded. Release Rafael now, and we will let you live."

Lucas exchanged a glance with Elena, who shook her head slightly. "He won't let us live," she whispered.

Lucas nodded, his grip tightening on the rifle. "We're not surrendering. We've got Rafael. If you want him alive, you'll back off."

There was a long pause, the silence stretching out uncomfortably. Finally, Gabriel's voice crackled over the bullhorn again. "You're playing a dangerous game, Detective. Don't make me do something we'll both regret."

"We have your son, and we'll use him if we have to," Lucas shouted back.

He looked over at Rafael, who was now lying flat on the floor, trying to make himself as small as possible.

"James, cover the back. Elena, keep an eye on Rafael and the side window. I'll take the front," Lucas said.

The three of them moved into position, the tension mounting with each passing second. Gabriel's men moved closer, their weapons ready, but they hesitated, wary of making the first move.

Suddenly, a shot rang out, shattering the silence. Lucas flinched, his finger tightening on the trigger. One of Gabriel's men crumpled to the ground, taken out by a well-placed shot from James.

"All hell's about to break loose," James muttered.

The air was filled with the deafening roar of gunfire as both sides opened up. Bullets tore through the wooden walls, splintering the furniture and sending shards of wood flying. Lucas fired back, aiming and picking off targets as they appeared. Gabriel's men moved with military precision, their tactical gear blending into the swamp's dense foliage.

Elena crouched by the window, her rifle spitting out rounds. "They're trying to flank us!" she shouted.

"Stay down!" Lucas shouted to Rafael, who lay flat on the floor, his face pale with fear.

"We can't let them get inside," James called from the back door, his rifle blasting out rounds that echoed through the house.

The battle raged on, the air thick with smoke and the acrid smell of gunpowder. Lucas felt a bullet whiz past his ear, the close call heightening his focus.

The gunfire outside the house ceased suddenly, leaving an eerie silence in its wake. Lucas, Elena, and James held their breath, their hearts pounding as they waited.

Without warning, both the front door and back door exploded inward, the force of the blasts sending wooden splinters and debris flying through the air. Lucas felt a searing pain as fragments tore into his skin, and he saw Elena, James, and Rafael reel from the impact, all sustaining minor injuries.

Before they could recover, two gunmen stormed through the front door, their automatic rifles blazing. At the same moment, two more gunmen burst through the back door, adding to the chaos. The house was filled with the deafening roar of gunfire, bullets tearing through the walls and furniture.

Lucas ducked behind the overturned wooden table, firing his rifle at the intruders. His shots were precise, and one of the gunmen crumpled to the floor, a dark stain spreading across his head.

Elena, positioned near the side window, returned fire. One of the gunmen from the back door fell, clutching his neck as he went down.

James stood his ground near the back door and his rifle roared. The other attacker from the back door was thrown back by the impact, his body hitting the floor with a sickening thud.

The remaining gunman, realizing he was outmatched, tried to retreat, but Lucas was faster. He fired a final shot, the bullet striking the man in the head. The house fell silent once more, the only sound the labored breathing of its occupants.

James staggered, his face contorted with pain as he clutched his thigh. Blood seeped through his fingers, staining his jeans a dark red. "Damn it! I'm hit," he gasped, his voice strained.

"Hold on, James," Lucas shouted.

James sat on the floor, his face was pale, and his breathing labored.

Elena scanned the room for something to use as a makeshift bandage. She spotted a small towel hanging on a hook by the kitchen sink and grabbed it, rushing to James's side.

"Hold still," she said. She wrapped the towel tightly around his thigh, just above the wound, creating a tourniquet to stem the bleeding. "You need to put pressure on the wound," she instructed, pressing his hands against the towel. "Like this."

James nodded, wincing in pain.

Lucas, positioned near the front door, felt a cold dread as he realized his rifle was out of bullets. The empty magazine clicked uselessly, and he cursed under his breath. He tossed the rifle to the floor and drew his Glock. "Elena, stay with James."

"Be careful," Elena said, her voice tight with concern.

Lucas glanced at the front door, hearing movement outside. "We're not done yet," he said grimly. "More are coming."

Lucas sprinted to the front door, his Glock at the ready. He burst through the shattered remnants of the door and into the yard, where two more gunmen were attempting to enter the house.

The men raised their rifles, but Lucas was faster. He dropped to one knee, his shots ringing out in rapid succession. The first gunman went down, his weapon clattering to the ground. The second managed to fire a burst, but the bullets went wide, missing Lucas by inches. Lucas squeezed the trigger, the final shot dropping the second man where he stood.

Breathing heavily, Lucas scanned the perimeter, his eyes sharp for any more threats. Satisfied that they were momentarily secure, he turned and hurried back into the house.

Inside, Elena was applying pressure to James's wound. Rafael sat nearby, his hands bound, his expression one of shock and fear.

"James, are you alright?" Lucas asked.

"James needs medical attention. When is the backup coming?" Elena asked.

"Damn it!" James cursed. "I'm still in the game," he grunted.

Through the shattered front door, Lucas saw a figure step forward, hands raised in a gesture of surrender. Gabriel's voice rang out. "Ceasefire! I want to talk!"

"What does he want now?" Elena muttered.

They watched as Gabriel pushed a young man forward, his hands tied behind his back. Lucas recognized him immediately—Miguel. Miguel's face was pale and bruised, his eyes wide with fear and confusion.

"Look who I found," Gabriel said, a cold smile playing on his lips. "Your brother, Detective Torres. I'm willing to make a trade—Miguel for Rafael."

Elena recognized the lean build, the curly hair that had never been tamed, no matter how hard their mother had tried.

"Miguel..." Elena's voice cracked, her grip tightening on her rifle.

"Let my brother go! He has nothing to do with this," Elena shouted.

Gabriel's smile widened, his eyes glittering with malice. "You have five minutes to decide. After that, the shooting resumes, and I can't guarantee Miguel's safety."

Lucas felt a surge of anger and frustration. The sight of Miguel, terrified and vulnerable, tore at his heart. He turned to Elena, his voice low. "Help should be here any minute." He knew as well as she did that deals with devils never ended well.

Elena nodded, her eyes filled with pain.

As the five minutes elapsed, Gabriel's voice rang out again, sharper and more menacing. "Time's up! What's your answer?"

Elena stood, her shoulders squared, her eyes locked onto Gabriel's. "No deal," she shouted. "We're not trading Rafael."

Gabriel's smile faded, replaced by a mask of cold fury. "Very well. You've made your choice. Open fire!"

The air exploded with the sound of gunfire as Gabriel's men opened up. Lucas ducked behind the overturned table.

He fired back, his shots precise and controlled, each one aimed to keep the attackers at bay.

Elena, positioned near the side window, fired in quick succession. "We need to hold them off," she shouted over the din. "We can't let them get inside again."

James, despite his injury, fired his rifle from his position near the back door, his face contorted with pain and effort. "We will keep them back!"

Amidst the thick smoke, Lucas felt a sharp sting as a bullet grazed his arm, but he kept firing. He took out one of Gabriel's men who had ventured too close to the house.

Chapter 30

Lucas, Elena, and James were holding their ground, but the distant roar of an airboat echoed through the swamp, signaling the arrival of more of Gabriel's crew.

Inside the battered house, Lucas and Elena gathered guns and ammunition from the bodies of the fallen gunmen.

Elena rummaged through the gear of a downed attacker, pulling out extra magazines and passing them to Lucas. "We're running low," she said, her voice tight with urgency. "This won't last us long."

Lucas nodded. He pulled out the satellite phone and dialed Captain Rodriguez's number. The line crackled to life, and Rodriguez's voice came through. "Lucas, what's your status?"

"Captain, we're almost out of ammunition. We can't hold them off much longer. What should we do?"

There was a brief pause before Rodriguez replied. "Help is on the way, Lucas. ETA is twenty minutes. Can you hold out until then?"

Lucas glanced at Elena, who was reloading her weapon. "We can hold for twenty more minutes."

As if sensing their communication, Gabriel's crew intensified their assault, bullets tearing through the walls and sending debris flying. Lucas and Elena fired back, their shots calculated and deadly, but the sheer volume of incoming fire was overwhelming.

Suddenly, an RPG whistled through the air and slammed into the side of the house. The explosion was deafening, a concussive blast that sent Lucas, Elena, James, and Rafael flying. The world spun in a chaotic blur, pain flaring in Lucas's shoulder as he hit the floor. Elena cried out, clutching her arm, while Rafael screamed in agony, blood pouring from the stumps where his fingers had been. James' eyes rolled into the back of his head, his body limp and motionless on the floor. Blood seeped from a gash on his forehead, mixing with debris around him.

Smoke filled the house and flames licked at the walls, casting a hellish glow. Lucas struggled to his feet, his vision swimming, his shoulder a throbbing mass of pain. He reached for the automatic rifle at his side, the weapon heavy in his hands.

"Elena!" he shouted, his voice hoarse. "Are you OK?"

"I'm all right," Elena said, her face contorted with pain.

She staggered to her feet, grabbed Rafael, and pulled him to a safer spot behind the sofa. "Stay low!" she instructed.

Two gunmen burst through the front door in a blur of black clothing and glinting weapons. Their faces were obscured by masks, as they scanned the room for their targets. Lucas stood in their way, his arm raised with the rifle. In a split second, gunfire pierced the air and all three figures fell to the floor. A red stain grew on Lucas' arm from where he was shot.

"Lucas, are you all right?" Elena shouted, clearly panicking.

Lucas felt a wave of desperation wash over him. They were outnumbered, outgunned, and running out of time. Just as the weight of their situation threatened to crush him, a new sound broke through the chaos—the unmistakable thrum of helicopter blades.

A police helicopter swooped into view. The mounted machine gun opened up, and a hail of bullets tore into Gabriel's crew. The tide of the battle shifted as the attackers scrambled for cover.

"Help is here!" Lucas shouted.

Gabriel's men began to retreat. From the loudspeaker mounted on the helicopter, a commanding voice echoed across the swamp.

"This is the police! Drop your weapons and lie down on the ground! This is your final warning!"

For a moment, there was a tense pause as Gabriel's men hesitated, their eyes darting between the imposing aircraft and their ruthless leader. A couple of gunmen, desperate and defiant, raised their weapons and fired at the helicopter. The response was swift and brutal. The machine gun on the helicopter roared to life, a hail of bullets blasting the attackers off their feet and sending them sprawling onto the ground.

The remaining gunmen began to drop their weapons. One by one, they laid their rifles and handguns aside, raising their hands in surrender before lying down on the grass, their faces pressed into the earth.

Several police officers descended from the helicopter on ropes. They quickly handcuffed the gunmen who had surrendered.

Amid the chaos, a few gunmen made a desperate dash for one of the airboats. They scrambled aboard and started the engine, the boat lurching forward as they sped away into the dense swamp.

Gabriel turned and ran toward the dock. His eyes were wild and his breath came in ragged gasps. Miguel, his hands tied behind his back, saw his chance. Summoning all his strength, he lunged forward and head-butted Gabriel, catching him off guard. Gabriel stumbled and fell to the ground, dazed.

A police officer rushed forward and pinned Gabriel to the ground, twisting his arms behind his back and securing him with handcuffs. Gabriel struggled, but the fight had gone out of him. The officer hauled him to his feet.

"Gabriel Sandoval, you are under arrest. You have the right to remain silent. Anything you say can and will be used against you in a court of law."

Lucas and Elena emerged from the battered house, supporting each other. Lucas's shoulder and arm were bandaged hastily, and Elena cradled her injured arm.

"Miguel!" Elena called, her voice breaking with relief. She rushed to her brother, who was being treated by a paramedic for his injuries.

"I'm okay," Miguel assured her.

Lucas joined them, his gaze shifting to Gabriel, now in police custody. "We got him," he said, his voice filled with a mix of exhaustion and triumph.

The calm after the storm was punctuated by the hum of approaching engines. Two large police airboats glided toward the dock. Medical staff disembarked from the airboats, moving with efficiency. They lift James onto a stretcher, his face pale and his breathing labored. Despite his weakened state, James managed to offer a faint smile as they secured him in place.

Captain Rodriguez stepped off one of the airboats and walked over to Lucas and Elena, her gaze sweeping over the scene of destruction before settling on them.

"You did an incredible job," Rodriguez said. "You held your ground against overwhelming odds and brought Gabriel Sandoval to justice. The department and the city owe you a great debt."

"We couldn't have done it without the backup, Captain. It was a team effort," Lucas said.

Elena, cradling her injured arm, gave a tired but grateful smile. "Thank you, Captain. We did what we had to do."

The medical team attended to the injuries of Lucas, Elena, and Rafael. Lucas couldn't help but flinch as they cleaned and covered his wounds. Elena's arm was carefully placed in a supportive sling, while Rafael's hand was wrapped in bandages.

"We need to get you all to a hospital," one of the medics said. "Let's get you onto the airboat."

Lucas, Elena, and Rafael were helped onto one of the airboats. Rodriguez walked alongside the airboat as it prepared to depart. "We'll clean up here and make sure Gabriel and his men are secured. You focus on getting better. We have a lot to discuss once you're back on your feet."

Lucas nodded. "Thank you, Captain."

Elena reached out and squeezed Rodriguez's hand. "We'll be back soon."

The airboat's engine roared to life, and they began to move away from the dock. Lucas looked back at the house, now a scene of devastation. He walked to James' stretcher, knelt, and held his hand. "How are you doing, brother?"

"I'll make it," James declared.

"I'm sure you will. I owe you big time, and I'll make sure you get a new house," Lucas said.

"Happy to be of help, brother."

Chapter 31

Entering Captain Rodriguez's office, Lucas and Elena moved carefully, mindful of their injuries. Bandages peeked out from beneath their clothing as they tried to avoid causing themselves more pain. The captain glanced up from her desk, a broad smile spreading across her face at the sight of them. She rose to greet them warmly. "Lucas, Elena, it's wonderful to see you both on your feet. Please, have a seat."

They took their seats, the effort causing a wince from Lucas as his shoulder protested the movement. Elena settled into her chair with a slight grimace, her arm still in a sling.

"I want to start by commending you both for your exceptional work in securing Rafael and arresting Gabriel Sandoval," Rodriguez began. "Thanks to your bravery and determination, we were able to dismantle a significant part of Gabriel's operation. I'm also pleased to inform you that, following your efforts, we've arrested several more of Gabriel's associates and confiscated drugs worth millions of dollars."

Elena's eyes widened with satisfaction. "That's great news, Captain. We've been fighting this battle for so long—it's good to see such a significant victory."

Rodriguez's smile broadened. "Lucas, for your outstanding leadership and bravery, you're being promoted to Sergeant."

Lucas blinked in surprise. "Thank you, Captain. It's an honor."

Rodriguez turned to Elena. "And Elena, for your exceptional detective work and dedication, you're being promoted to Senior Detective."

Elena's face lit up. "Thank you, Captain. I am deeply grateful."

"Captain, has the department identified the mole?" Lucas asked.

Rodriguez's expression darkened slightly. "Yes, we have. It was a desk sergeant who was on Gabriel's payroll. He's been arrested and is cooperating with the investigation."

Lucas nodded. "I'm glad we've rooted him out. It was a dangerous breach."

Rodriguez's expression softened as she turned to Elena. "Elena, I have some good news regarding your brother Miguel. He's been cleared of any charges. His cooperation in helping us arrest Gabriel was invaluable."

Elena's eyes filled with tears of relief. "Thank you, Captain. That means the world to me."

"He's free now, and with your guidance, I'm sure he'll stay on the right path," Rodriguez said.

As Lucas and Elena stood to leave, Rodriguez extended her hand. "Congratulations to both of you. The department is lucky to have you."

Lucas and Elena shook her hand, gratitude and pride shining in their eyes.

Chapter 32

The sun hung high in the clear, azure sky, casting its golden rays over the sparkling waters of the Miami coastline. The ocean stretched out in a mesmerizing expanse of deep blue. Gentle waves rolled in, their rhythmic lapping creating a soothing melody that blended with the distant calls of seagulls. On the beach, powdery white sand stretched for miles. Palm trees lined the edge of the beach, their fronds swaying gently in the sea breeze.

Lucas, Elena, and Ava found a perfect spot near the water's edge, where the sand was cool and slightly damp. They set up their beach umbrella. Lucas spread out a large beach towel, while Elena unpacked the cooler, filled with drinks and snacks to keep them refreshed throughout the day.

Ava was a bundle of energy. Her curly brown hair was tied back in pigtails, and her eyes sparkled with delight as she took in the vast ocean before her. She wore a bright pink swimsuit adorned with little seashells, her tiny feet already half-buried in the sand.

"Daddy, look at the waves!" Ava exclaimed.

Lucas chuckled. "Do you want to build a sandcastle with Elena, princess?"

Ava nodded eagerly. "Yes, please!"

In a navy blue swimsuit, Elena knelt beside Ava, her smile mirroring the little girl's enthusiasm. "Alright, let's build a big sandcastle." She handed Ava a small plastic bucket and shovel, and together they began to shape the sand into towers and walls. Seeing Elena and Ava get along so well brought Lucas immense joy.

As they worked on the sandcastle, the waves continued their gentle dance, occasionally sending a refreshing spray their way.

Elena and Ava's sandcastle grew taller, adorned with seashells and tiny flags made from bits of driftwood.

"Daddy, look!" Ava called out, her face beaming with pride. "We made a castle!"

Lucas smiled, kneeling to admire their creation. "It's amazing, Ava."

"We make a pretty good team," Elena said softly, her hand gently brushing Ava's hair.

Lucas nodded. "Yes, you do."

"Do you want to learn how to swim, princess?" Lucas asked.

"Yes, Daddy! I want to swim like a fish!"

They waded into the shallow water, the coolness a refreshing contrast to the warm sand. Ava giggled as the waves lapped at her legs, her fear melting away in the presence of her father and Elena. Lucas knelt in the water, holding Ava as she floated on her back, her little arms flailing with excitement.

"Just relax and let the water support you," Lucas said. "You're doing great, Ava."

Elena joined them, her hands gently guiding Ava's arms. "Kick your legs, just like this," she demonstrated. Ava mimicked her, kicking her legs and laughing as the water splashed around them. Ava's confidence grew with each passing moment. Lucas and Elena took turns holding her, their hands guiding her movements.

Lucas turned to Elena. "Thank you for today, Elena. It's been perfect."

"I wouldn't have missed it for the world. Ava is such a wonderful little girl. You're doing a great job with her, Lucas."

Their gazes locked, and the world around them seemed to fade away. Lucas reached out, his hand gently cupping Elena's cheek. She leaned into his touch, her eyes closing briefly before meeting his again.

"I love you, Elena," Lucas whispered.

Elena's breath hitched, her heart pounding in her chest. "I love you too, Lucas."

Without another word, they moved closer, their arms wrapping around each other in a tight embrace. Their lips met in a passionate kiss.

Ava's giggles brought them back to the present, and they broke apart, smiling down at the little girl who had been watching them with a big grin. "Daddy and Elena are kissing!" she exclaimed, clapping her hands in delight.

"Yes, we are," Lucas said, lifting Ava into his arms. "And we're going to be very happy together."

www.ingramcontent.com/pod-product-compliance
Lightning Source LLC
LaVergne TN
LVHW041811060526
838201LV00046B/1209